THE LEGEND
OF SLEEPY
HOLLOW

WASHINGTON IRVING

This edition published 2004 by Geddes & Grosset,
David Dale House, New Lanark, ML11 9DJ, Scotland

This edition © 2004 Geddes & Grosset

ISBN 1 84205 503 8

Printed and bound in Poland

Contents

The Legend of Sleepy Hollow

Found among the Papers of the Late Diedrich Knickerbocker

> A pleasing land of drowsy head it was,
> Of dreams that wave before the half-shut eye;
> And of gay castles in the clouds that pass,
> Forever flushing round a summer sky.
> *Castle of Indolence*

IN THE bosom of one of those spacious coves which indent the eastern shore of the Hudson, at that broad expansion of the river denominated by the ancient Dutch navigators the Tappan Zee, and where they always prudently shortened sail and implored the protection of St. Nicholas when they crossed, there lies a small market town or rural port, which by some is called Greensburgh, but which is more generally and properly known by the name of Tarry Town. This name was given, we are told, in former days, by the good housewives of the adjacent country, from the inveterate propensity of their husbands to linger about the village tavern on market days. Be that as it may, I do not vouch for the fact, but merely advert to it, for the sake of being precise and authentic. Not far from this village, perhaps about two miles, there is a little valley or rather lap of land among high hills, which is one of the quietest places in the whole world. A small brook glides through it, with just murmur enough to lull one to repose; and the occasional whistle of a quail or tapping of a woodpecker is almost the only sound that ever breaks in upon the uniform tranquillity.

I recollect that, when a stripling, my first exploit in squirrel-shooting was in a grove of tall walnut-trees that shades one side of the valley. I had wandered into it at noontime, when all nature is peculiarly quiet, and was startled by the roar of my own gun, as it broke the Sabbath stillness around and was prolonged and reverberated by the angry echoes. If ever I should wish for a retreat whither I might steal from the world and its distractions, and dream quietly away the remnant of a troubled life, I know of none more promising than this little valley.

From the listless repose of the place, and the peculiar character of its inhabitants, who are descendants from the original Dutch settlers, this sequestered glen has long been known by the name of Sleepy Hollow, and its rustic lads are called the Sleepy Hollow Boys throughout all the neighboring country. A drowsy, dreamy influence seems to hang over the land, and to pervade the very atmosphere. Some say that the place was bewitched by a High German doctor, during the early days of the settlement; others, that an old Indian chief, the prophet or wizard of his tribe, held his powwows there before the country was discovered by Master Hendrick Hudson. Certain it is, the place still continues under the sway of some witching power, that holds a spell over the minds of the good people, causing them to walk in a continual reverie. They are given to all kinds of marvellous beliefs, are subject to trances and visions, and frequently see strange sights, and hear music and voices in the air. The whole neighborhood abounds with local tales, haunted spots, and twilight superstitions; stars shoot and meteors glare oftener across the valley than in any other part of the country, and the nightmare, with her whole ninefold, seems to make it the favorite scene of her gambols.

The dominant spirit, however, that haunts this enchanted region, and seems to be commander-in-chief of all the powers of the air, is the apparition of a figure on horseback, without a head. It is said by some to be the ghost of a Hessian trooper, whose head had been carried away by a cannon-ball, in some nameless battle during the Revolutionary War, and who is ever and anon seen by the country folk hurrying along in the gloom of night, as if on the wings of the wind. His haunts are not confined to the valley, but extend at times to the adjacent roads, and especially to the vicinity of a church at no great distance. Indeed, certain of the most authentic historians of those parts, who have been careful in collecting and collating the floating facts concerning this spectre, allege that the body of the trooper having been buried in the churchyard, the ghost rides forth to the scene of battle in nightly quest of his head, and that the rushing speed with which he sometimes passes along the Hollow, like a midnight blast, is owing to his being belated, and in a hurry to get back to the churchyard before daybreak.

Such is the general purport of this legendary superstition, which has furnished materials for many a wild story in that region of shadows; and the spectre is known at all the country firesides, by the name of the Headless Horseman of Sleepy Hollow.

It is remarkable that the visionary propensity I have mentioned is not confined to the native inhabitants of the valley, but is unconsciously imbibed by every one who resides there for a time. However wide awake they may have been before they entered that sleepy region, they are sure, in a little time, to inhale the witching influence of the air, and begin to grow imaginative, to dream dreams, and see apparitions.

I mention this peaceful spot with all possible laud, for it is in such little retired Dutch valleys, found here and there embosomed in the great State of New York, that population, manners, and customs remain fixed, while the great torrent of migration and improvement, which is making such incessant changes in other parts of this restless country, sweeps by them unobserved. They are like those little nooks of still water, which border a rapid stream, where we may see the straw and bubble riding quietly at anchor, or slowly revolving in their mimic harbor, undisturbed by the rush of the passing current. Though many years have elapsed since I trod the drowsy shades of Sleepy Hollow, yet I question whether I should not still find the same trees and the same families vegetating in its sheltered bosom.

In this by-place of nature there abode, in a remote period of American history, that is to say, some thirty years since, a worthy wight of the name of Ichabod Crane, who sojourned, or, as he expressed it, "tarried," in Sleepy Hollow, for the purpose of instructing the children of the vicinity. He was a native of Connecticut, a State which supplies the Union with pioneers for the mind as well as for the forest, and sends forth yearly its legions of frontier woodmen and country schoolmasters. The cognomen of Crane was not inapplicable to his person. He was tall, but exceedingly lank, with narrow shoulders, long arms and legs, hands that dangled a mile out of his sleeves, feet that might have served for shovels, and his whole frame most loosely hung together. His head was small, and flat at top, with huge ears, large green glassy eyes, and a long snipe nose, so that it looked like a weather-cock perched upon his spindle neck to tell which way the wind blew. To see him striding along the profile of a hill on a windy day, with his clothes bagging and fluttering about him, one might have mistaken him for the genius of famine descending upon the earth, or some scarecrow eloped from a cornfield.

His schoolhouse was a low building of one large room, rudely constructed of logs; the windows partly glazed, and partly patched with leaves of old copybooks. It was most ingeniously secured at vacant hours, by a withe twisted in the handle of the door, and stakes set against the window shutters; so that though a thief might get in with perfect ease, he would find some embarrassment in getting out,—an idea most probably borrowed by the architect, Yost Van Houten, from the mystery of an eelpot. The schoolhouse stood in a rather lonely but pleasant situation, just at the foot of a woody hill, with a brook running close by, and a formidable birch-tree growing at one end of it. From hence the low murmur of his pupils' voices, conning over their lessons, might be heard in a drowsy summer's day, like the hum of a beehive; interrupted now and then by the authoritative voice of the master, in the tone of menace or command, or, peradventure, by the appalling sound of the birch, as he urged some tardy loiterer along the flowery path of knowledge. Truth to say, he was a conscientious man, and ever bore in mind the golden maxim, "Spare the rod and spoil the child." Ichabod Crane's scholars certainly were not spoiled.

I would not have it imagined, however, that he was one of those cruel potentates of the school who joy in the smart of their subjects; on the contrary, he administered justice with discrimination rather than severity; taking the burden off the backs of the weak, and laying it on those of the strong. Your mere puny stripling, that winced at the least flourish of the rod, was passed by with indulgence; but the claims of justice were satisfied by inflicting a double portion on some little tough wrong-headed, broad-skirted Dutch urchin, who sulked and swelled and grew dogged and sullen beneath the birch. All this he called "doing his duty by their parents;" and he never inflicted a chastisement without following it by the assurance, so consolatory to the smarting urchin, that "he would remember it and thank him for it the longest day he had to live."

When school hours were over, he was even the companion and playmate of the larger boys; and on holiday afternoons would convoy some of the smaller ones home, who happened to have pretty sisters, or good housewives for mothers, noted for the comforts of the cupboard. Indeed, it behooved him to keep on good terms with his pupils. The revenue arising from his school was small, and would have been scarcely sufficient to furnish him with daily bread, for he was a huge feeder, and, though lank, had the dilating powers of an anaconda; but to help out his maintenance, he was, according to country custom in those parts, boarded and lodged at the houses of the farmers whose children he instructed. With these he lived successively a week at a time, thus going the rounds of the neighborhood, with all his worldly effects tied up in a cotton handkerchief.

That all this might not be too onerous on the purses of his rustic patrons, who are apt to consider the costs of schooling a grievous burden, and schoolmasters as mere drones, he had various ways of rendering himself both useful and agreeable. He assisted the farmers occasionally in the lighter labors of their farms, helped to make hay, mended the fences, took the horses to water, drove the cows from pasture, and cut wood for the winter fire. He laid aside, too, all the dominant dignity and absolute sway with which he lorded it in his little empire, the school, and became wonderfully gentle and ingratiating. He found favor in the eyes of the mothers by petting the children, particularly the youngest; and like the lion bold, which whilom so magnanimously the lamb did hold, he would sit with a child on one knee, and rock a cradle with his foot for whole hours together.

In addition to his other vocations, he was the singing-master of the neighborhood, and picked up many bright shillings by instructing the young folks in psalmody. It was a matter of no little vanity to him on Sundays, to take his station in front of the church gallery, with a band of chosen singers; where, in his own mind, he completely carried away the palm from the parson. Certain it is, his voice resounded far above all the rest of the congregation; and there are peculiar quavers still to be heard in that church, and which may even be heard half a mile off, quite to the opposite side of the millpond, on a still Sunday morning, which are said to be legitimately descended from the nose of Ichabod Crane. Thus, by divers little makeshifts, in that ingenious way which is commonly denominated "by hook and by crook," the worthy pedagogue got on tolerably enough, and was thought, by all who understood nothing of the labor of headwork, to have a wonderfully easy life of it.

The schoolmaster is generally a man of some importance in the female circle of a rural neighborhood; being considered a kind of idle, gentlemanlike personage, of vastly superior taste and accomplishments to the rough country swains, and, indeed, inferior in learning only to the parson. His appearance, therefore, is apt to occasion some little stir at the tea-table of a farmhouse, and the addition of a supernumerary dish of cakes or sweetmeats, or, peradventure, the parade of a silver teapot. Our man of letters, therefore, was peculiarly happy in the smiles of all the country damsels. How he would figure among them in the churchyard, between services on Sundays; gathering grapes for them from the wild vines that overran the surrounding trees; reciting for their amusement all the epitaphs on the tombstones; or sauntering, with a whole bevy of them, along the banks of the adjacent millpond; while the more bashful country bumpkins hung sheepishly back, envying his superior elegance and address.

From his half-itinerant life, also, he was a kind of travelling gazette, carrying the whole budget of local gossip from house to house, so that his appearance was always greeted with satisfaction. He was, moreover, esteemed by the women as a man of great erudition, for he had read several books quite through, and was a perfect master of Cotton Mather's History of *New England Witchcraft*, in which, by the way, he most firmly and potently believed.

He was, in fact, an odd mixture of small shrewdness and simple credulity. His appetite for the marvellous, and his powers of digesting it, were equally extraordinary; and both had been increased by his residence in this spell-bound region. No tale was too gross or monstrous for his capacious swallow. It was often his delight, after his school was dismissed in the afternoon, to stretch himself on the rich bed of clover bordering the little brook that whimpered by his schoolhouse, and there con over old Mather's direful tales, until the gathering dusk of evening made the printed page a mere mist before his eyes. Then, as he wended his way by swamp and stream and awful woodland, to the farmhouse where he happened to be quartered, every sound of nature, at that witching hour, fluttered his excited imagination,—the moan of the whippoorwill* from the hillside, the boding cry of the tree toad, that harbinger of storm, the dreary hooting of the screech owl, or the sudden rustling in the thicket of birds frightened from their roost. The fireflies, too, which sparkled most vividly in the darkest places, now and then startled him, as one of uncommon brightness would stream across his path; and if, by chance, a huge blockhead of a beetle came winging his blundering flight against him, the poor varlet was ready to give up the ghost, with the idea that he was struck with a witch's token. His only resource on such occasions, either to drown thought or drive away evil spirits, was to sing psalm tunes and the good people of Sleepy Hollow, as they sat by their doors of an evening, were often filled with awe at hearing his nasal melody, "in linked sweetness long drawn out," floating from the distant hill, or along the dusky road.

Another of his sources of fearful pleasure was to pass long winter evenings with the old Dutch wives, as they sat spinning by the fire, with a row of apples roasting and spluttering along the hearth, and listen to their marvellous tales of ghosts and goblins, and haunted fields, and haunted brooks, and haunted bridges, and

---

* The whippoorwill is a bird which is only heard at night. It receives its name from its note, which is thought to resemble those words.

haunted houses, and particularly of the headless horseman, or Galloping Hessian of the Hollow, as they sometimes called him. He would delight them equally by his anecdotes of witchcraft, and of the direful omens and portentous sights and sounds in the air, which prevailed in the earlier times of Connecticut; and would frighten them woefully with speculations upon comets and shooting stars; and with the alarming fact that the world did absolutely turn round, and that they were half the time topsy-turvy!

But if there was a pleasure in all this, while snugly cuddling in the chimney corner of a chamber that was all of a ruddy glow from the crackling wood fire, and where, of course, no spectre dared to show its face, it was dearly purchased by the terrors of his subsequent walk homewards. What fearful shapes and shadows beset his path, amidst the dim and ghastly glare of a snowy night! With what wistful look did he eye every trembling ray of light streaming across the waste fields from some distant window! How often was he appalled by some shrub covered with snow, which, like a sheeted spectre, beset his very path! How often did he shrink with curdling awe at the sound of his own steps on the frosty crust beneath his feet; and dread to look over his shoulder, lest he should behold some uncouth being tramping close behind him! And how often was he thrown into complete dismay by some rushing blast, howling among the trees, in the idea that it was the Galloping Hessian on one of his nightly scourings!

All these, however, were mere terrors of the night, phantoms of the mind that walk in darkness; and though he had seen many spectres in his time, and been more than once beset by Satan in divers shapes, in his lonely perambulations, yet daylight put an end to all these evils; and he would have passed a pleasant life of it, in despite of the Devil and all his works, if his path had not been crossed by a being that causes more perplexity to mortal man than ghosts, goblins, and the whole race of witches put together, and that was—a woman.

Among the musical disciples who assembled, one evening in each week, to receive his instructions in psalmody, was Katrina Van Tassel, the daughter and only child of a substantial Dutch farmer. She was a blooming lass of fresh eighteen; plump as a partridge; ripe and melting and rosy-cheeked as one of her father's peaches, and universally famed, not merely for her beauty, but her vast expectations. She was withal a little of a coquette, as might be perceived even in her dress, which was a mixture of ancient and modern fashions, as most suited to set off her charms. She wore the ornaments of pure yellow gold, which her great-great-grandmother had brought over from Saardam; the tempting stomacher of the olden time, and withal a provokingly short petticoat, to display the prettiest foot and ankle in the country round.

Ichabod Crane had a soft and foolish heart towards the sex; and it is not to be wondered at that so tempting a morsel soon found favor in his eyes, more especially after he had visited her in her paternal mansion. Old Baltus Van Tassel was a perfect picture of a thriving, contented, liberal-hearted farmer. He seldom, it is true, sent either his eyes or his thoughts beyond the boundaries of his own farm; but within those everything was snug, happy and well-conditioned. He was satisfied with his wealth, but not proud of it; and piqued himself upon the hearty abundance, rather than the style in which he lived. His stronghold was situated on the banks of the Hudson, in one of those green, sheltered, fertile nooks in which the Dutch farmers are so fond of nestling. A great elm tree spread its broad branches over it, at the foot of which bubbled up a spring of the softest and sweetest water, in a little well formed of a barrel; and then stole sparkling away through the grass, to a neighboring brook, that babbled along among alders and dwarf willows. Hard by the farmhouse was a vast barn, that might have served for a church; every window and crevice of which seemed bursting forth with the treasures of the farm; the flail was busily resounding within it from morning to night; swallows and martins skimmed twittering about the eaves; and rows of pigeons, some with one eye turned up, as if watching the weather, some with their heads under their wings or buried in their bosoms, and others swelling, and cooing, and bowing about their dames, were enjoying the sunshine on the roof. Sleek unwieldy porkers were grunting in the repose and abundance of their pens, from whence sallied forth, now and then, troops of sucking pigs, as if to snuff the air. A stately squadron of snowy geese were riding in an adjoining pond, convoying whole fleets of ducks; regiments of turkeys were gobbling through the farmyard, and Guinea fowls fretting about it, like ill-tempered housewives, with their peevish, discontented cry. Before the barn door strutted the gallant cock, that pattern of a husband, a warrior and a fine gentleman, clapping his burnished wings and crowing in the pride and gladness of his heart,—sometimes tearing up the earth with his feet, and then generously calling his ever-hungry family of wives and children to enjoy the rich morsel which he had discovered.

The pedagogue's mouth watered as he looked upon this sumptuous promise of luxurious winter fare. In his devouring mind's eye, he pictured to himself every roasting-pig running about with a pudding in his belly, and an apple in his mouth; the pigeons were snugly put to bed in a comfortable pie, and tucked in with a coverlet of crust; the geese were swimming in their own gravy; and the ducks pairing cosily in dishes, like snug married couples, with a decent competency of onion sauce. In the porkers he saw carved out the future sleek side of bacon, and juicy relishing ham; not a turkey but he beheld daintily trussed up, with its gizzard under its wing, and, peradventure, a necklace of savory sausages; and even bright chanticleer himself lay sprawling on his back, in a side dish, with uplifted claws, as if craving that quarter which his chivalrous spirit disdained to ask while living.

As the enraptured Ichabod fancied all this, and as he rolled his great green eyes over the fat meadow lands, the rich fields of wheat, of rye, of buckwheat, and Indian corn, and the orchards burdened with ruddy fruit, which surrounded the warm tenement of Van Tassel, his heart yearned after the damsel who was to inherit these domains, and his imagination expanded with the idea, how they might be readily turned into cash, and the money invested in immense tracts of wild land, and shingle palaces in the wilderness. Nay, his busy fancy already realized his hopes, and presented to him the blooming Katrina, with a whole family of children, mounted on the top of a wagon loaded with household trumpery, with pots and kettles dangling beneath; and he beheld himself bestriding a pacing mare, with a colt at her heels, setting out for Kentucky, Tennessee,—or the Lord knows where!

When he entered the house, the conquest of his heart was complete. It was one of those spacious farmhouses, with high-ridged but lowly sloping roofs, built in the style handed down from the first Dutch settlers; the low projecting eaves forming a piazza along the front, capable of being closed up in bad weather. Under this were hung flails, harness, various utensils of husbandry, and nets for fishing in the neighboring river. Benches were built along the sides for summer use; and a great spinning-wheel at one end, and a churn at the other, showed the various uses to which this important porch might be devoted. From this piazza the wondering Ichabod entered the hall, which formed the centre of the mansion, and the place of usual residence. Here rows of resplendent pewter, ranged on a long dresser, dazzled his eyes. In one corner stood a huge bag of wool, ready to be spun; in another, a quantity of linsey-woolsey just from the loom; ears of Indian corn, and strings of dried apples and peaches, hung in gay festoons along the walls, mingled with the gaud of red peppers; and a door left ajar gave him a peep into the best parlor, where the claw-footed chairs and dark mahogany tables shone like mirrors; andirons, with their accompanying shovel and tongs, glistened from their covert of asparagus tops; mock-oranges and conch-shells decorated the mantelpiece; strings of various-colored birds eggs were suspended above it; a great ostrich egg was hung from the centre of the room, and a corner cupboard, knowingly left open, displayed immense treasures of old silver and well-mended china.

From the moment Ichabod laid his eyes upon these regions of delight, the peace of his mind was at an end, and his only study was how to gain the affections of the peerless daughter of Van Tassel. In this enterprise, however, he had more real difficulties than generally fell to the lot of a knight-errant of yore, who seldom had anything but giants, enchanters, fiery dragons, and such like easily conquered adversaries, to contend with and had to make his way merely through gates of iron and brass, and walls of adamant to the castle keep, where the lady of his heart was confined; all which he achieved as easily as a man would carve his way to the centre of a Christmas pie; and then the lady gave him her hand as a matter of course. Ichabod, on the contrary, had to win his way to the heart of a country coquette, beset with a labyrinth of whims and caprices, which were forever presenting new difficulties and impediments; and he had to encounter a host of fearful adversaries of real flesh and blood, the numerous rustic admirers, who beset every portal to her heart, keeping a watchful and angry eye upon each other, but ready to fly out in the common cause against any new competitor.

Among these, the most formidable was a burly, roaring, roystering blade, of the name of Abraham, or, according to the Dutch abbreviation, Brom Van Brunt, the hero of the country round, which rang with his feats of strength and hardihood. He was broad-shouldered and double-jointed, with short curly black hair, and a bluff but not unpleasant countenance, having a mingled air of fun and arrogance. From his Herculean frame and great powers of limb he had received the nickname of BROM BONES, by which he was universally known. He was famed for great knowledge and skill in horsemanship, being as dexterous on horseback as a Tartar. He was foremost at all races and cock fights; and, with the ascendancy which bodily strength always acquires in rustic life, was the umpire in all disputes, setting his hat on one side, and giving his decisions with an air and tone that admitted of no gainsay or appeal. He was always ready for either a fight or a frolic; but had more mischief than ill-will in his composition; and with all his overbearing roughness, there was a strong dash of waggish good humor at bottom. He had three or four boon companions, who regarded him as their model, and at the head of whom he scoured the country, attending every scene of feud or merriment for miles round. In cold weather he was distinguished by a fur cap, surmounted with a flaunting fox's tail; and when the folks at a country gathering descried this well-known crest at a distance, whisking about among a squad of hard riders, they always stood by for a squall. Sometimes his crew would be heard dashing along past the farmhouses at midnight, with whoop and halloo, like a troop of Don Cossacks; and the old dames, startled out of their sleep, would listen for a moment till the hurry-scurry had clattered by, and then exclaim, "Ay, there goes Brom Bones and his gang!" The neighbors looked upon him with a mixture of awe, admiration, and good-will; and, when any madcap prank or rustic brawl occurred in the vicinity, always shook their heads, and warranted Brom Bones was at the bottom of it.

This rantipole hero had for some time singled out the blooming Katrina for the object of his uncouth gallantries, and though his amorous toyings were something like the gentle caresses and endearments of a bear, yet it was whispered that she did not altogether discourage his hopes. Certain it is, his advances were signals for rival candidates to retire, who felt no inclination to cross a lion in his amours; insomuch, that when his horse was seen tied to Van Tassel's paling, on a Sunday night, a sure sign that his master was courting, or, as it is termed, "sparking," within, all other suitors passed by in despair, and carried the war into other quarters.

Such was the formidable rival with whom Ichabod Crane had to contend, and, considering all things, a stouter man than he would have shrunk from the competition, and a wiser man would have despaired. He had, however, a happy mixture of pliability and perseverance in his nature; he was in form and spirit like a supple-jack—yielding, but tough; though he bent, he never broke; and though he bowed beneath the slightest pressure, yet, the moment it was away—jerk!—he was as erect, and carried his head as high as ever.

To have taken the field openly against his rival would have been madness; for he was not a man to be thwarted in his amours, any more than that stormy lover, Achilles. Ichabod, therefore, made his advances in a quiet and gently insinuating manner. Under cover of his character of singing-master, he made frequent visits at the farmhouse; not that he had anything to apprehend from the meddlesome interference of parents, which is so often a stumbling-block in the path of lovers. Balt Van Tassel was an easy indulgent soul; he loved his daughter better even than his pipe, and, like a reasonable man and an excellent father, let her have her way in everything. His notable little wife, too, had enough to do to attend to her housekeeping and manage her poultry; for, as she sagely observed, ducks and geese are foolish things, and must be looked after, but girls can take care of themselves. Thus, while the busy dame bustled about the house, or plied her spinning-wheel at one end of the piazza, honest Balt would sit smoking his evening pipe at the other, watching the achievements of a little wooden warrior, who, armed with a sword in each hand, was most valiantly fighting the wind on the pinnacle of the barn. In the mean time, Ichabod would carry on his suit with the daughter by the side of the spring under the great elm, or sauntering along in the twilight, that hour so favorable to the lover's eloquence.

I profess not to know how women's hearts are wooed and won. To me they have always been matters of riddle and admiration. Some seem to have but one vulnerable point, or door of access; while others have a thousand avenues, and may be captured in a thousand different ways. It is a great triumph of skill to gain the former, but a still greater proof of generalship to maintain possession of the latter, for man must battle for his fortress at every door and window. He who wins a thousand common hearts is therefore entitled to some renown; but he who keeps undisputed sway over the heart of a coquette is indeed a hero. Certain it is, this was not the case with the redoubtable Brom Bones; and from the moment Ichabod Crane made his advances, the interests of the former evidently declined: his horse was no longer seen tied to the palings on Sunday nights, and a deadly feud gradually arose between him and the preceptor of Sleepy Hollow.

Brom, who had a degree of rough chivalry in his nature, would fain have carried matters to open warfare and have settled their pretensions to the lady, according to the mode of those most concise and simple reasoners, the knights-errant of yore— by single combat; but Ichabod was too conscious of the superior might of his adversary to enter the lists against him; he had overheard a boast of Bones, that he would "double the schoolmaster up, and lay him on a shelf of his own schoolhouse;" and he was too wary to give him an opportunity. There was something extremely provoking in this obstinately pacific system; it left Brom no alternative but to draw upon the funds of rustic waggery in his disposition, and to play off boorish practical jokes upon his rival. Ichabod became the object of whimsical persecution to Bones and his gang of rough riders. They harried his hitherto peaceful domains; smoked out his singing school by stopping up the chimney; broke into the schoolhouse at night, in spite of its formidable fastenings of withe and window stakes, and turned everything topsy-turvy, so that the poor schoolmaster began to think all the witches in the country held their meetings there. But what was still more annoying, Brom took all opportunities of turning him into ridicule in presence of his mistress, and had a scoundrel dog whom he taught to whine in the most ludicrous manner, and introduced as a rival of Ichabod's, to instruct her in psalmody.

In this way matters went on for some time, without producing any material effect on the relative situations of the contending powers. On a fine autumnal afternoon, Ichabod, in pensive mood, sat enthroned on the lofty stool from whence he usually watched all the concerns of his little literary realm. In his hand he swayed a ferule, that sceptre of despotic power; the birch of justice reposed on three nails behind the throne, a constant terror to evil doers, while on the desk before him might be seen sundry contraband articles and prohibited weapons, detected upon the persons of idle urchins, such as half-munched apples, popguns, whirligigs, fly-cages, and whole legions of rampant little paper gamecocks. Apparently there had been some appalling act of justice recently inflicted, for his scholars were all busily intent upon their books, or slyly whispering behind them with one eye kept upon the master; and a kind of buzzing stillness reigned throughout the schoolroom. It was suddenly interrupted by the appearance of a negro in tow-cloth jacket and trowsers, a round-crowned fragment of a hat, like the cap of Mercury, and mounted on the back of a ragged, wild, half-broken colt, which he managed with a rope by way of halter. He came clattering up to the school door with an invitation to Ichabod to attend a merry-making or "quilting frolic," to be held that evening at Mynheer Van Tassel's; and having delivered his message with that air of importance, and effort at fine language, which a negro is apt to display on petty embassies of the kind, he dashed over the brook, and was seen scampering away up the hollow, full of the importance and hurry of his mission.

All was now bustle and hubbub in the late quiet schoolroom. The scholars were hurried through their lessons without stopping at trifles; those who were nimble skipped over half with impunity, and those who were tardy had a smart application now and then in the rear, to quicken their speed or help them over a tall word. Books were flung aside without being put away on the shelves, inkstands were overturned, benches thrown down, and the whole school was turned loose an hour before the usual time, bursting forth like a legion of young imps, yelping and racketing about the green in joy at their early emancipation.

The gallant Ichabod now spent at least an extra half hour at his toilet, brushing and furbishing up his best, and indeed only suit of rusty black, and arranging his locks by a bit of broken looking-glass that hung up in the schoolhouse. That he might make his appearance before his mistress in the true style of a cavalier, he borrowed a horse from the farmer with whom he was domiciliated, a choleric old Dutchman of the name of Hans Van Ripper, and, thus gallantly mounted, issued forth like a knight-errant in quest of adventures. But it is meet I should, in the true spirit of romantic story, give some account of the looks and equipments of my hero and his steed. The animal he bestrode was a broken-down plow-horse, that had outlived almost everything but its viciousness. He was gaunt and shagged, with a ewe neck, and a head like a hammer; his rusty mane and tail were tangled and knotted with burs; one eye had lost its pupil, and was glaring and spectral, but the other had the gleam of a genuine devil in it. Still he must have had fire and mettle in his day, if we may judge from the name he bore of Gunpowder. He had, in fact, been a favorite steed of his master's, the choleric Van Ripper, who was a furious rider, and had infused, very probably, some of his own spirit into the animal; for, old and broken-down as he looked, there was more of the lurking devil in him than in any young filly in the country.

Ichabod was a suitable figure for such a steed. He rode with short stirrups, which brought his knees nearly up to the pommel of the saddle; his sharp elbows stuck out like grasshoppers'; he carried his whip perpendicularly in his hand, like a sceptre, and as his horse jogged on, the motion of his arms was not unlike the flapping of a pair of wings. A small wool hat rested on the top of his nose, for so his scanty strip of forehead might be called, and the skirts of his black coat fluttered out almost to the horses tail. Such was the appearance of Ichabod and his steed as they shambled out of the gate of Hans Van Ripper, and it was altogether such an apparition as is seldom to be met with in broad daylight.

It was, as I have said, a fine autumnal day; the sky was clear and serene, and nature wore that rich and golden livery which we always associate with the idea of abundance. The forests had put on their sober brown and yellow, while some trees of the tenderer kind had been nipped by the frosts into brilliant dyes of orange, purple, and scarlet. Streaming files of wild ducks began to make their appearance high in the air; the bark of the squirrel might be heard from the groves of beech and hickory-nuts, and the pensive whistle of the quail at intervals from the neighboring stubble field.

The small birds were taking their farewell banquets. In the fullness of their revelry, they fluttered, chirping and frolicking from bush to bush, and tree to tree, capricious from the very profusion and variety around them. There was the honest cock robin, the favorite game of stripling sportsmen, with its loud querulous note; and the twittering blackbirds flying in sable clouds; and the golden-winged woodpecker with his crimson crest, his broad black gorget, and splendid plumage; and the cedar bird, with its red-tipt wings and yellow-tipt tail and its little monteiro cap of feathers; and the blue jay, that noisy coxcomb, in his gay light blue coat and white underclothes, screaming and chattering, nodding and bobbing and bowing, and pretending to be on good terms with every songster of the grove.

As Ichabod jogged slowly on his way, his eye, ever open to every symptom of culinary abundance, ranged with delight over the treasures of jolly autumn. On all sides he beheld vast store of apples; some hanging in oppressive opulence on the trees; some gathered into baskets and barrels for the market; others heaped up in rich piles for the cider-press. Farther on he beheld great fields of Indian corn, with its golden ears peeping from their leafy coverts, and holding out the promise of cakes and hasty-pudding; and the yellow pumpkins lying beneath them, turning up their fair round bellies to the sun, and giving ample prospects of the most luxurious of pies; and anon he passed the fragrant buckwheat fields breathing the odor of the beehive, and as he beheld them, soft anticipations stole over his mind of dainty slapjacks, well buttered, and garnished with honey or treacle, by the delicate little dimpled hand of Katrina Van Tassel.

Thus feeding his mind with many sweet thoughts and "sugared suppositions," he journeyed along the sides of a range of hills which look out upon some of the goodliest scenes of the mighty Hudson. The sun gradually wheeled his broad disk down in the west. The wide bosom of the Tappan Zee lay motionless and glassy, excepting that here and there a gentle undulation waved and prolonged the blue shadow of the distant mountain. A few amber clouds floated in the sky, without a breath of air to move them. The horizon was of a fine golden tint, changing gradually into a pure apple green, and from that into the deep blue of the mid-heaven. A slanting ray lingered on the woody crests of the precipices that overhung some parts of the river, giving greater depth to the dark gray and purple of their rocky sides. A sloop was loitering in the distance, dropping slowly down with the tide, her sail hanging uselessly against the mast; and as the reflection of the sky gleamed along the still water, it seemed as if the vessel was suspended in the air.

It was toward evening that Ichabod arrived at the castle of the Heer Van Tassel, which he found thronged with the pride and flower of the adjacent country. Old farmers, a spare leathern-faced race, in homespun coats and breeches, blue stockings, huge shoes, and magnificent pewter buckles. Their brisk, withered little dames, in close-crimped caps, long-waisted short gowns, homespun petticoats, with scissors and pincushions, and gay calico pockets hanging on the outside. Buxom lasses, almost as antiquated as their mothers, excepting where a straw hat, a fine ribbon, or perhaps a white frock, gave symptoms of city innovation. The sons, in short square-skirted coats, with rows of stupendous brass buttons, and their hair generally queued in the fashion of the times, especially if they could procure an eel-skin for the purpose, it being esteemed throughout the country as a potent nourisher and strengthener of the hair.

Brom Bones, however, was the hero of the scene, having come to the gathering on his favorite steed Daredevil, a creature, like himself, full of mettle and mischief, and which no one but himself could manage. He was, in fact, noted for preferring vicious animals, given to all kinds of tricks which kept the rider in constant risk of his neck, for he held a tractable, well-broken horse as unworthy of a lad of spirit.

Fain would I pause to dwell upon the world of charms that

burst upon the enraptured gaze of my hero, as he entered the state parlor of Van Tassel's mansion. Not those of the bevy of buxom lasses, with their luxurious display of red and white; but the ample charms of a genuine Dutch country tea-table, in the sumptuous time of autumn. Such heaped up platters of cakes of various and almost indescribable kinds, known only to experienced Dutch housewives! There was the doughty dough-nut, the tender oly koek, and the crisp and crumbling cruller; sweet cakes and short cakes, ginger cakes and honey cakes, and the whole family of cakes. And then there were apple pies, and peach pies, and pumpkin pies; besides slices of ham and smoked beef; and moreover delectable dishes of preserved plums, and peaches, and pears, and quinces; not to mention broiled shad and roasted chickens; together with bowls of milk and cream, all mingled higgledy-piggledy, pretty much as I have enumerated them, with the motherly teapot sending up its clouds of vapor from the midst— Heaven bless the mark! I want breath and time to discuss this banquet as it deserves, and am too eager to get on with my story. Happily, Ichabod Crane was not in so great a hurry as his historian, but did ample justice to every dainty.

He was a kind and thankful creature, whose heart dilated in proportion as his skin was filled with good cheer, and whose spirits rose with eating, as some men's do with drink. He could not help, too, rolling his large eyes round him as he ate, and chuckling with the possibility that he might one day be lord of all this scene of almost unimaginable luxury and splendor. Then, he thought, how soon he'd turn his back upon the old school-house; snap his fingers in the face of Hans Van Ripper, and every other niggardly patron, and kick any itinerant pedagogue out of doors that should dare to call him comrade!

Old Baltus Van Tassel moved about among his guests with a face dilated with content and good humor, round and jolly as the harvest moon. His hospitable attentions were brief, but expressive, being confined to a shake of the hand, a slap on the shoulder, a loud laugh, and a pressing invitation to "fall to, and help themselves."

And now the sound of the music from the common room, or hall, summoned to the dance. The musician was an old gray-headed negro, who had been the itinerant orchestra of the neighborhood for more than half a century. His instrument was as old and battered as himself. The greater part of the time he scraped on two or three strings, accompanying every movement of the bow with a motion of the head; bowing almost to the ground, and stamping with his foot whenever a fresh couple were to start.

Ichabod prided himself upon his dancing as much as upon his vocal powers. Not a limb, not a fibre about him was idle; and to have seen his loosely hung frame in full motion, and clattering about the room, you would have thought St. Vitus himself, that blessed patron of the dance, was figuring before you in person. He was the admiration of all the negroes; who, having gathered, of all ages and sizes, from the farm and the neighborhood, stood forming a pyramid of shining black faces at every door and window, gazing with delight at the scene, rolling their white eyeballs, and showing grinning rows of ivory from ear to ear. How could the flogger of urchins be otherwise than animated and joyous? The lady of his heart was his partner in the dance, and smiling graciously in reply to all his amorous oglings; while Brom Bones, sorely smitten with love and jealousy, sat brooding by himself in one corner.

When the dance was at an end, Ichabod was attracted to a knot of the sager folks, who, with Old Van Tassel, sat smoking at one end of the piazza, gossiping over former times, and drawing out long stories about the war.

This neighborhood, at the time of which I am speaking, was one of those highly favored places which abound with chronicle and great men. The British and American line had run near it during the war; it had, therefore, been the scene of marauding and infested with refugees, cowboys, and all kinds of border chivalry. Just sufficient time had elapsed to enable each story-teller to dress up his tale with a little becoming fiction, and, in the indistinctness of his recollection, to make himself the hero of every exploit.

There was the story of Doffue Martling, a large blue-bearded Dutchman, who had nearly taken a British frigate with an old iron nine-pounder from a mud breastwork, only that his gun burst at the sixth discharge. And there was an old gentleman who shall be nameless, being too rich a mynheer to be lightly mentioned, who, in the battle of White Plains, being an excel-lent master of defence, parried a musket-ball with a small sword, insomuch that he absolutely felt it whiz round the blade, and glance off at the hilt; in proof of which he was ready at any time to show the sword, with the hilt a little bent. There were sev-eral more that had been equally great in the field, not one of whom but was persuaded that he had a considerable hand in bringing the war to a happy termination.

But all these were nothing to the tales of ghosts and appari-tions that succeeded. The neighborhood is rich in legendary treasures of the kind. Local tales and superstitions thrive best in these sheltered, long-settled retreats; but are trampled under foot by the shifting throng that forms the population of most of our country places. Besides, there is no encourage-ment for ghosts in most of our villages, for they have scarcely had time to finish their first nap and turn themselves in their graves, before their surviving friends have travelled away from the neighborhood; so that when they turn out at night to walk their rounds, they have no acquaintance left to call upon. This is perhaps the reason why we so seldom hear of ghosts except in our long-established Dutch communities.

The immediate cause, however, of the prevalence of super-natural stories in these parts, was doubtless owing to the vicinity of Sleepy Hollow. There was a contagion in the very air that blew from that haunted region; it breathed forth an atmosphere of dreams and fancies infecting all the land. Several of the Sleepy Hollow people were present at Van Tassel's, and, as usual, were doling out their wild and wonderful legends. Many dismal tales were told about funeral trains, and mourning cries and wailings heard and seen about the great tree where the unfortunate Major André was taken, and which stood in the neighborhood. Some mention was made also of the woman in white, that haunted the dark glen at Raven Rock, and was often heard to shriek on winter nights before a storm, having perished there in the snow. The chief part of the stories, however, turned upon the favorite spectre of Sleepy Hollow, the Headless Horseman, who had been heard several times of late, patrolling the country; and, it was said, tethered his horse nightly among the graves in the churchyard.

The sequestered situation of this church seems always to have made it a favorite haunt of troubled spirits. It stands on a knoll, surrounded by locust-trees and lofty elms, from among which its decent, whitewashed walls shine modestly forth, like Christian purity beaming through the shades of retirement. A gentle slope descends from it to a silver sheet of water, bordered by high trees, between which, peeps may be caught at the blue hills of the Hudson. To look upon its grass-grown yard, where the sunbeams seem to sleep so quietly, one would think that there at least the dead might rest in peace. On one side of the church extends a wide woody dell, along which raves a large brook among broken rocks and trunks of fallen trees. Over a deep black part of the stream, not far from the church, was formerly thrown a wooden bridge; the road that led to it, and the bridge itself, were thickly shaded by overhanging trees, which cast a gloom about it, even in the daytime; but occasioned a fearful darkness at night. Such was one of the favorite haunts of the Headless Horseman, and the place where he was most frequently encountered. The tale was told of old Brouwer, a most heretical disbeliever in ghosts, how he met the Horseman returning from his foray into Sleepy Hollow, and was obliged to get up behind him; how they galloped over bush and brake, over hill and swamp, until they reached the bridge; when the Horseman suddenly turned into a skeleton, threw old Brouwer into the brook, and sprang away over the tree-tops with a clap of thunder.

This story was immediately matched by a thrice marvellous adventure of Brom Bones, who made light of the Galloping Hessian as an arrant jockey. He affirmed that on returning one night from the neighboring village of Sing Sing, he had been overtaken by this midnight trooper; that he had offered to race with him for a bowl of punch, and should have won it too, for Daredevil beat the goblin horse all hollow, but just as they came to the church bridge, the Hessian bolted, and vanished in a flash of fire.

All these tales, told in that drowsy undertone with which men talk in the dark, the countenances of the listeners only now and then receiving a casual gleam from the glare of a pipe, sank deep in the mind of Ichabod. He repaid them in kind with large extracts from his invaluable author, Cotton Mather, and added many marvellous events that had taken place in his native State of Connecticut, and fearful sights which he had seen in his nightly walks about Sleepy Hollow.

The revel now gradually broke up. The old farmers gathered together their families in their wagons, and were heard for some time rattling along the hollow roads, and over the distant hills. Some of the damsels mounted on pillions behind their favorite swains, and their light-hearted laughter, mingling with the clatter of hoofs, echoed along the silent woodlands, sounding fainter and fainter, until they gradually died away,—and the late scene of noise and frolic was all silent and deserted. Ichabod only lingered behind, according to the custom of country lovers, to have a tête-à-tête with the heiress; fully convinced that he was now on the high road to success. What passed at this interview I will not pretend to say, for in fact I do not know. Something, however, I fear me, must have gone wrong, for he certainly sallied forth, after no very great interval, with an air quite desolate and chapfallen. Oh, these women! these women! Could that girl have been playing off any of her coquettish tricks? Was her encouragement of the poor pedagogue all a mere sham to secure her conquest of his rival? Heaven only knows, not I! Let it suffice to say, Ichabod stole forth with the air of one who had been sacking a henroost, rather than a fair lady's heart. Without looking to the right or left to notice the scene of rural wealth, on which he had so often gloated, he went straight to the stable, and with several hearty cuffs and kicks roused his steed most uncourteously from the comfortable quarters in which he was soundly sleeping, dreaming of mountains of corn and oats, and whole valleys of timothy and clover.

It was the very witching time of night that Ichabod, heavy-hearted and crestfallen, pursued his travels homewards, along the sides of the lofty hills which rise above Tarry Town, and which he had traversed so cheerily in the afternoon. The hour was as dismal as himself. Far below him the Tappan Zee spread its dusky and indistinct waste of waters, with here and there the tall mast of a sloop, riding quietly at anchor under the land. In the dead hush of midnight, he could even hear the barking of the watchdog from the opposite shore of the Hudson; but it was so vague and faint as only to give an idea of his distance from this faithful companion of man. Now and then, too, the long-drawn crowing of a cock, accidentally awakened, would

sound far, far off, from some farmhouse away among the hills—
but it was like a dreaming sound in his ear. No signs of life
occurred near him, but occasionally the melancholy chirp of a
cricket, or perhaps the guttural twang of a bullfrog from a
neighboring marsh, as if sleeping uncomfortably and turning
suddenly in his bed.

All the stories of ghosts and goblins that he had heard in the
afternoon now came crowding upon his recollection. The night
grew darker and darker; the stars seemed to sink deeper in the
sky, and driving clouds occasionally hid them from his sight.
He had never felt so lonely and dismal. He was, moreover, approaching the very place where many of the scenes of the ghost
stories had been laid. In the centre of the road stood an enormous tulip-tree, which towered like a giant above all the other
trees of the neighborhood, and formed a kind of landmark. Its
limbs were gnarled and fantastic, large enough to form trunks
for ordinary trees, twisting down almost to the earth, and rising
again into the air. It was connected with the tragical story of the
unfortunate André, who had been taken prisoner hard by; and
was universally known by the name of Major André's tree.
The common people regarded it with a mixture of respect and
superstition, partly out of sympathy for the fate of its ill-starred
namesake, and partly from the tales of strange sights, and doleful
lamentations, told concerning it.

As Ichabod approached this fearful tree, he began to whistle; he thought his whistle was answered; it was but a blast
sweeping sharply through the dry branches. As he approached
a little nearer, he thought he saw something white, hanging in
the midst of the tree: he paused and ceased whistling but, on
looking more narrowly, perceived that it was a place where the
tree had been scathed by lightning, and the white wood laid
bare. Suddenly he heard a groan—his teeth chattered, and his
knees smote against the saddle: it was but the rubbing of one

huge bough upon another, as they were swayed about by the breeze. He passed the tree in safety, but new perils lay before him.

About two hundred yards from the tree, a small brook crossed the road, and ran into a marshy and thickly-wooded glen, known by the name of Wiley's Swamp. A few rough logs, laid side by side, served for a bridge over this stream. On that side of the road where the brook entered the wood, a group of oaks and chestnuts, matted thick with wild grape-vines, threw a cavernous gloom over it. To pass this bridge was the severest trial. It was at this identical spot that the unfortunate André was captured, and under the covert of those chestnuts and vines were the sturdy yeomen concealed who surprised him. This has ever since been considered a haunted stream, and fearful are the feelings of the schoolboy who has to pass it alone after dark.

As he approached the stream, his heart began to thump; he summoned up, however, all his resolution, gave his horse half a score of kicks in the ribs, and attempted to dash briskly across the bridge; but instead of starting forward, the perverse old animal made a lateral movement, and ran broadside against the fence. Ichabod, whose fears increased with the delay, jerked the reins on the other side, and kicked lustily with the contrary foot: it was all in vain; his steed started, it is true, but it was only to plunge to the opposite side of the road into a thicket of brambles and alder bushes. The schoolmaster now bestowed both whip and heel upon the starveling ribs of old Gunpowder, who dashed forward, snuffling and snorting, but came to a stand just by the bridge, with a suddenness that had nearly sent his rider sprawling over his head. Just at this moment a plashy tramp by the side of the bridge caught the sensitive ear of Ichabod. In the dark shadow of the grove, on the margin of the brook, he beheld something huge, misshapen and towering. It stirred not, but seemed gathered up in the gloom, like some gigantic monster ready to spring upon the traveller.

The hair of the affrighted pedagogue rose upon his head with terror. What was to be done? To turn and fly was now too late; and besides, what chance was there of escaping ghost or goblin, if such it was, which could ride upon the wings of the wind? Summoning up, therefore, a show of courage, he demanded in stammering accents, "Who are you?" He received no reply. He repeated his demand in a still more agitated voice. Still there was no answer. Once more he cudgelled the sides of the inflexible Gunpowder, and, shutting his eyes, broke forth with involuntary fervor into a psalm tune. Just then the shadowy object of alarm put itself in motion, and with a scramble and a bound stood at once in the middle of the road. Though the night was dark and dismal, yet the form of the unknown might now in some degree be ascertained. He appeared to be a horseman of large dimensions, and mounted on a black horse of powerful frame. He made no offer of molestation or sociability, but kept aloof on one side of the road, jogging along on the blind side of old Gunpowder, who had now got over his fright and waywardness.

Ichabod, who had no relish for this strange midnight companion, and bethought himself of the adventure of Brom Bones with the Galloping Hessian, now quickened his steed in hopes of leaving him behind. The stranger, however, quickened his horse to an equal pace. Ichabod pulled up, and fell into a walk, thinking to lag behind—the other did the same. His heart began to sink within him; he endeavored to resume his psalm tune, but his parched tongue clove to the roof of his mouth, and he could not utter a stave. There was something in the moody and dogged silence of this pertinacious companion that was mysterious and appalling. It was soon fearfully accounted for. On mounting a rising ground, which brought the figure of his fellow-traveller in relief against the sky, gigantic in height, and muffled in a cloak, Ichabod was horror-struck on perceiving that he was headless!—but his horror was still more increased on observing that the head, which should have rested on his shoulders, was carried before him on the pommel of his saddle! His terror rose to desperation; he rained a shower of kicks and blows upon Gunpowder, hoping by a sudden movement to give his companion the slip; but the spectre started full jump with him. Away, then, they dashed through thick and thin; stones flying and sparks flashing at every bound. Ichabod's flimsy garments fluttered in the air, as he stretched his long lank body away over his horse's head, in the eagerness of his flight.

They had now reached the road which turns off to Sleepy Hollow; but Gunpowder, who seemed possessed with a demon, instead of keeping up it, made an opposite turn, and plunged headlong downhill to the left. This road leads through a sandy hollow shaded by trees for about a quarter of a mile, where it crosses the bridge famous in goblin story; and just beyond swells the green knoll on which stands the whitewashed church.

As yet the panic of the steed had given his unskilful rider an apparent advantage in the chase, but just as he had got half way through the hollow, the girths of the saddle gave way, and he felt it slipping from under him. He seized it by the pommel, and endeavored to hold it firm, but in vain; and had just time to save himself by clasping old Gunpowder round the neck, when the saddle fell to the earth, and he heard it trampled under foot by his pursuer. For a moment the terror of Hans Van Ripper's wrath passed across his mind,—for it was his Sunday saddle; but this was no time for petty fears; the goblin was hard on his haunches; and (unskilful rider that he was!) he had much ado to maintain his seat; sometimes slipping on one side, sometimes on another, and sometimes jolted on the high ridge of his horse's backbone, with a violence that he verily feared would cleave him asunder.

An opening in the trees now cheered him with the hopes that the church bridge was at hand. The wavering reflection of a silver star in the bosom of the brook told him that he was not mistaken. He saw the walls of the church dimly glaring under the trees beyond. He recollected the place where Brom Bones's ghostly competitor had disappeared. "If I can but reach that bridge," thought Ichabod, "I am safe." Just then he heard the black steed panting and blowing close behind him; he even fancied that he felt his hot breath. Another convulsive kick in the ribs, and old Gunpowder sprang upon the bridge; he thundered over the resounding planks; he gained the opposite side; and now Ichabod cast a look behind to see if his pursuer should vanish, according to rule, in a flash of fire and brimstone. Just then he saw the goblin rising in his stirrups, and in the very act of hurling his head at him. Ichabod endeavored to dodge the horrible missile, but too late. It encountered his cranium with a tremendous crash—he was tumbled headlong into the dust, and Gunpowder, the black steed, and the goblin rider, passed by like a whirlwind.

The next morning the old horse was found without his saddle, and with the bridle under his feet, soberly cropping the grass at his master's gate. Ichabod did not make his appearance at breakfast; dinner-hour came, but no Ichabod. The boys assembled at the schoolhouse, and strolled idly about the banks of the brook; but no schoolmaster. Hans Van Ripper now began to feel some uneasiness about the fate of poor Ichabod, and his saddle. An inquiry was set on foot, and after diligent investigation they came upon his traces. In one part of the road leading to the church was found the saddle trampled in the dirt; the tracks of horses' hoofs deeply dented in the road, and evidently at furious speed, were traced to the bridge, beyond which, on the bank of a broad part of the brook, where the water ran deep and black, was found the hat of the unfortunate Ichabod, and close beside it a shattered pumpkin.

The brook was searched, but the body of the schoolmaster was not to be discovered. Hans Van Ripper as executor of his estate, examined the bundle which contained all his worldly effects. They consisted of two shirts and a half; two stocks for the neck; a pair or two of worsted stockings; an old pair of corduroy small-clothes; a rusty razor; a book of psalm tunes full of dog's-ears; and a broken pitch-pipe. As to the books and furniture of the schoolhouse, they belonged to the community, excepting Cotton Mather's *History of Witchcraft*, a *New England Almanac*, and a book of dreams and fortune-telling; in which last was a sheet of foolscap much scribbled and blotted in several fruitless attempts to make a copy of verses in honor of the heiress of Van Tassel. These magic books and the poetic scrawl were forthwith consigned to the flames by Hans Van Ripper; who, from that time forward, determined to send his children no more to school, observing that he never knew any good come of this same reading and writing. Whatever money the schoolmaster possessed, and he had received his quarter's pay but a day or two before, he must have had about his person at the time of his disappearance.

The mysterious event caused much speculation at the church on the following Sunday. Knots of gazers and gossips were collected in the churchyard, at the bridge, and at the spot where the hat and pumpkin had been found. The stories of Brouwer, of Bones, and a whole budget of others were called to mind; and when they had diligently considered them all, and compared them with the symptoms of the present case, they shook their heads, and came to the conclusion that Ichabod had been carried off by the Galloping Hessian. As he was a bachelor, and in nobody's debt, nobody troubled his head any more about him; the school was removed to a different quarter of the hollow, and another pedagogue reigned in his stead.

It is true, an old farmer, who had been down to New York on a visit several years after, and from whom this account of the ghostly adventure was received, brought home the intelligence that Ichabod Crane was still alive; that he had left the neighborhood partly through fear of the goblin and Hans Van Ripper, and partly in mortification at having been suddenly dismissed by the heiress; that he had changed his quarters to a distant part of the country; had kept school and studied law at the same time; had been admitted to the bar; turned politician; electioneered; written for the newspapers; and finally had been made a justice of the Ten Pound Court. Brom Bones, too, who, shortly after his rival's disappearance conducted the blooming Katrina in triumph to the altar, was observed to look exceedingly knowing whenever the story of Ichabod was related, and always burst into a hearty laugh at the mention of the pumpkin; which led some to suspect that he knew more about the matter than he chose to tell.

The old country wives, however, who are the best judges of these matters, maintain to this day that Ichabod was spirited away by supernatural means; and it is a favorite story often told about the neighborhood round the winter evening fire. The bridge became more than ever an object of superstitious awe; and that may be the reason why the road has been altered of late years, so as to approach the church by the border of the millpond. The schoolhouse being deserted soon fell to decay, and was reported to be haunted by the ghost of the unfortunate pedagogue and the plowboy, loitering shomeward of a still summer evening, has often fancied his voice at a distance, chanting a melancholy psalm tune among the tranquil solitudes of Sleepy Hollow.

Rip Van Winkle

A Posthumous Writing of Diedrich Knickerbocker

By Woden, God of Saxons,
From whence comes Wensday, that is Wodensday.
Truth is a thing that ever I will keep
Unto thylke day in which I creep into
My sepulchre—

Cartwright

*　　*　　*　　*　　*　　*　　*　　*

THE FOLLOWING Tale was found among the papers of the late Diedrich Knickerbocker, an old gentleman of New York, who was very curious in the Dutch history of the province, and the manners of the descendants from its primitive settlers. His historical researches, however, did not lie so much among books as among men; for the former are lamentably scanty on his favorite topics; whereas he found the old burghers, and still more their wives, rich in that legendary lore, so invaluable to true history. Whenever, therefore, he happened upon a genuine Dutch family, snugly shut up in its low-roofed farmhouse, under a spreading sycamore, he looked upon it as a little clasped volume of black-letter, and studied it with the zeal of a book-worm.

The result of all these researches was a history of the province during the reign of the Dutch governors, which he published some years since. There have been various opinions as to the literary character of his work, and, to tell the truth, it is not a whit better than it should be. Its chief merit is its scrupulous accuracy, which indeed was a little questioned on its first appearance, but has since been completely established; and it is now admitted into all historical collections, as a book of unquestionable authority.

The old gentleman died shortly after the publication of his work, and now that he is dead and gone, it cannot do much harm to his memory to say that his time might have been much better employed in weightier labors. He, however, was apt to ride his hobby his own way; and though it did now and then kick up the dust a little in the eyes of his neighbors, and grieve the spirit of some friends, for whom he felt the truest deference and affection; yet his errors and follies are remembered "more in sorrow than in anger," and it begins to be suspected, that he never intended to injure or offend. But however his memory may be appreciated by critics, it is still held dear by many folk, whose good opinion is well worth having; particularly by certain biscuit-bakers, who have gone so far as to imprint his likeness on their new-year cakes; and have thus given him a chance for immortality, almost equal to the being stamped on a Waterloo Medal, or a Queen Anne's Farthing.

*　　*　　*　　*　　*　　*　　*　　*

WHOEVER has made a voyage up the Hudson must remember the Kaatskill mountains. They are a dis membered branch of the great Appalachian family, and are seen away to the west of the river, swelling up to a noble height, and lording it over the surrounding country. Every change of season, every change of weather, indeed, every hour of the day, produces some change in the magical hues and shapes of these mountains, and they are regarded by all the goodwives, far and near, as perfect barometers. When the weather is fair and settled, they are clothed in blue and purple, and print their bold outlines on the clear evening sky; but, sometimes, when the rest of the landscape is cloudless, they will gather a hood of gray vapors about their summits, which, in the last rays of the setting sun, will glow and light up like a crown of glory.

At the foot of these fair mountains, the voyager may have descried the light smoke curling up from a village, whose shingle-roofs gleam among the trees, just where the blue tints of the upland melt away into the fresh green of the nearer landscape. It is a little village, of great antiquity, having been founded by some of the Dutch colonists, in the early times of the province, just about the beginning of the government of the good Peter Stuyvesant, (may he rest in peace!) and there were some of the houses of the original settlers standing within a few years, built of small yellow bricks brought from Holland, having latticed windows and gable fronts, surmounted with weather-cocks.

In that same village, and in one of these very houses (which, to tell the precise truth, was sadly time-worn and weather-beaten), there lived many years since, while the country was yet a province of Great Britain, a simple good-natured fellow, of the name of Rip Van Winkle. He was a descendant of the Van Winkles who figured so gallantly in the chivalrous days of Peter Stuyvesant, and accompanied him to the siege of Fort Christina. He inherited, however, but little of the martial character of his ancestors. I have observed that he was a simple good-natured man; he was, moreover, a kind neighbor, and an obedient hen-pecked husband. Indeed, to the latter circumstance might be owing that meekness of spirit which gained him such universal popularity; for those men are most apt to be obsequious and conciliating abroad, who are under the discipline of shrews at home. Their tempers, doubtless, are rendered pliant and malleable in the fiery furnace of domestic tribulation; and a curtain lecture is worth all the sermons in the world for teaching the virtues of patience and long-suffering. A termagant wife may, therefore, in some respects, be considered a tolerable blessing; and if so, Rip Van Winkle was thrice blessed.

Certain it is, that he was a great favorite among all the good wives of the village, who, as usual, with the amiable sex, took his part in all family squabbles; and never failed, whenever they talked those matters over in their evening gossipings, to lay all the blame on Dame Van Winkle. The children of the village, too, would shout with joy whenever he approached. He assisted at their sports, made their playthings, taught them to fly kites and shoot marbles, and told them long stories of ghosts, witches, and Indians. Whenever he went dodging about the village, he was surrounded by a troop of them, hanging on his skirts, clambering on his back, and playing a thousand tricks on him with impunity; and not a dog would bark at him throughout the neighborhood.

The great error in Rip's composition was an insuperable aversion to all kinds of profitable labor. It could not be from the want of assiduity or perseverance; for he would sit on a wet rock, with a rod as long and heavy as a Tartar's lance, and fish all day without a murmur, even though he should not be encouraged by a single nibble. He would carry a fowling-piece on his shoulder for hours together, trudging through woods and swamps, and up hill and down dale, to shoot a few squirrels or wild pigeons. He would never refuse to assist a neighbor even in the roughest toil, and was a foremost man at all country frolics for husking Indian corn, or building stone-fences; the women of the village, too, used to employ him to run their errands, and to do such little odd jobs as their less obliging husbands would not do for them. In a word Rip was ready to attend to anybody's business but his own; but as to doing family duty, and keeping his farm in order, he found it impossible.

In fact, he declared it was of no use to work on his farm; it was the most pestilent little piece of ground in the whole country; every thing about it went wrong, and would go wrong, in spite of him. His fences were continually falling to pieces; his cow would either go astray, or get among the cabbages; weeds were sure to grow quicker in his fields than anywhere else; the rain always made a point of setting in just as he had some outdoor work to do; so that though his patrimonial estate had dwindled away under his management, acre by acre, until there was little more left than a mere patch of Indian corn and potatoes, yet it was the worst conditioned farm in the neighborhood.

His children, too, were as ragged and wild as if they belonged to nobody. His son Rip, an urchin begotten in his own likeness, promised to inherit the habits, with the old clothes of his father. He was generally seen trooping like a colt at his mother's heels, equipped in a pair of his father's cast-off galligaskins, which he had much ado to hold up with one hand, as a fine lady does her train in bad weather.

Rip Van Winkle, however, was one of those happy mortals, of foolish, well-oiled dispositions, who take the world easy, eat white bread or brown, whichever can be got with least thought or trouble, and would rather starve on a penny than work for a pound. If left to himself, he would have whistled life away in perfect contentment; but his wife kept continually dinning in his ears about his idleness, his carelessness, and the ruin he was bringing on his family. Morning, noon, and night, her tongue was incessantly going, and every thing he said or did was sure to produce a torrent of household eloquence. Rip had but one way of replying to all lectures of the kind, and that, by frequent use, had grown into a habit. He shrugged his shoulders, shook his head, cast up his eyes, but said nothing. This, however, always provoked a fresh volley from his wife; so that he was fain to draw off his forces, and take to the outside of the house—the only side which, in truth, belongs to a hen-pecked husband.

Rip's sole domestic adherent was his dog Wolf, who was as much hen-pecked as his master; for Dame Van Winkle regarded them as companions in idleness, and even looked upon Wolf with an evil eye, as the cause of his master's going so often astray. True it is, in

all points of spirit befitting an honorable dog, he was as coura-
geous an animal as ever scoured the woods—but what courage
can withstand the ever-during and all-besetting terrors of a woman's tongue? The moment Wolf entered the house his crest fell,
his tail drooped to the ground, or curled between his legs, he
sneaked about with a gallows air, casting many a sidelong glance at
Dame Van Winkle, and at the least flourish of a broomstick or la-
dle, he would fly to the door with yelping precipitation.

Times grew worse and worse with Rip Van Winkle as years of
matrimony rolled on; a tart temper never mellows with age, and
a sharp tongue is the only edged tool that grows keener with
constant use. For a long while he used to console himself, when
driven from home, by frequenting a kind of perpetual club of
the sages, philosophers, and other idle personages of the
village; which held its sessions on a bench before a small inn,
designated by a rubicund portrait of His Majesty George the
Third. Here they used to sit in the shade through a long lazy
summer's day, talking listlessly over village gossip, or telling end-
less sleepy stories about nothing. But it would have been worth
any statesman's money to have heard the profound discussions
that sometimes took place, when by chance an old newspaper
fell into their hands from some passing traveller. How solemnly
they would listen to the contents, as drawled out by Derrick
Van Bummel, the schoolmaster, a dapper learned little man,
who was not to be daunted by the most gigantic word in the dic-
tionary; and how sagely they would deliberate upon public events
some months after they had taken place.

The opinions of this junto were completely controlled by
Nicholas Vedder, a patriarch of the village, and landlord of the
inn, at the door of which he took his seat from morning till night
just moving sufficiently to avoid the sun and keep in the shade
of a large tree; so that the neighbors could tell the hour by his
movements as accurately as by a sun-dial. It is true he was rarely

heard to speak, but smoked his pipe incessantly. His adherents, however (for every great man has his adherents), perfectly understood him, and knew how to gather his opinions. When any thing that was read or related displeased him, he was observed to smoke his pipe vehemently, and to send forth short, frequent and angry puffs; but when pleased, he would inhale the smoke slowly and tranquilly, and emit it in light and placid clouds; and sometimes, taking the pipe from his mouth, and letting the fragrant vapor curl about his nose, would gravely nod his head in token of perfect approbation.

From even this stronghold the unlucky Rip was at length routed by his termagant wife, who would suddenly break in upon the tranquillity of the assemblage and call the members all to naught; nor was that august personage, Nicholas Vedder himself, sacred from the daring tongue of this terrible virago, who charged him outright with encouraging her husband in habits of idleness.

Poor Rip was at last reduced almost to despair; and his only alternative, to escape from the labor of the farm and clamor of his wife, was to take gun in hand and stroll away into the woods. Here he would sometimes seat himself at the foot of a tree, and share the contents of his wallet with Wolf, with whom he sympathized as a fellow-sufferer in persecution. "Poor Wolf," he would say, "thy mistress leads thee a dog's life of it; but never mind, my lad, whilst I live thou shalt never want a friend to stand by thee!" Wolf would wag his tail, look wistfully in his master's face, and if dogs can feel pity I verily believe he reciprocated the sentiment with all his heart.

In a long ramble of the kind on a fine autumnal day, Rip had unconsciously scrambled to one of the highest parts of the Kaatskill mountains. He was after his favorite sport of squirrel shooting, and the still solitudes had echoed and re-echoed with the reports of his gun. Panting and fatigued, he threw himself, late in the afternoon, on a green knoll, covered with mountain herbage, that crowned the brow of a precipice. From an opening between the trees he could overlook all the lower country for many a mile of rich woodland. He saw at a distance the lordly Hudson, far, far below him, moving on its silent but majestic course, with the reflection of a purple cloud, or the sail of a lagging bark, here and there sleeping on its glassy bosom, and at last losing itself in the blue highlands.

On the other side he looked down into a deep mountain glen, wild, lonely, and shagged, the bottom filled with fragments from the impending cliffs, and scarcely lighted by the reflected rays of the setting sun. For some time Rip lay musing on this scene; evening was gradually advancing; the mountains began to throw their long blue shadows over the valleys; he saw that it would be dark long before he could reach the village, and he heaved a heavy sigh when he thought of encountering the terrors of Dame Van Winkle.

As he was about to descend, he heard a voice from a distance, hallooing, "Rip Van Winkle! Rip Van Winkle!" He looked round, but could see nothing but a crow winging its solitary flight across the mountain. He thought his fancy must have deceived him, and turned again to descend, when he heard the same cry ring through the still evening air; "Rip Van Winkle! Rip Van Winkle!"— at the same time Wolf bristled up his back, and giving a low growl, skulked to his master's side, looking fearfully down into the glen. Rip now felt a vague apprehension stealing over him; he looked anxiously in the same direction, and perceived a strange figure slowly toiling up the rocks, and bending under the weight of something he carried on his back. He was surprised to see any human being in this lonely and unfrequented place, but supposing it to be some one of the neighborhood in need of his assistance, he hastened down to yield it.

On nearer approach he was still more surprised at the singularity of the stranger's appearance. He was a short square-built old fellow, with thick bushy hair, and a grizzled beard. His dress was of the antique Dutch fashion—a cloth jerkin strapped round the waist—several pair of breeches, the outer one of ample volume, decorated with rows of buttons down the sides, and bunches at the knees. He bore on his shoulder a stout keg, that seemed full of liquor, and made signs for Rip to approach and assist him with the load. Though rather shy and distrustful of this new acquaintance, Rip complied with his usual alacrity; and mutually relieving one another, they clambered up a narrow gully, apparently the dry bed of a mountain torrent. As they ascended, Rip every now and then heard long rolling peals, like distant thunder, that seemed to issue out of a deep ravine, or rather cleft, between lofty rocks, toward which their rugged path conducted. He paused for an instant, but supposing it to be the muttering of one of those transient thunder-showers which often take place in mountain heights, he proceeded. Passing through the ravine, they came to a hollow, like a small amphitheatre, surrounded by perpendicular precipices, over the brinks of which impending trees shot their branches, so that you only caught glimpses of the azure sky and the bright evening cloud. During the whole time Rip and his companion had labored on in silence; for though the former marvelled greatly what could be the object of carrying a keg of liquor up this wild mountain, yet there was something strange and incomprehensible about the unknown, that inspired awe and checked familiarity.

On entering the amphitheatre, new objects of wonder presented themselves. On a level spot in the centre was a company of odd-looking personages playing at nine-pins. They were dressed in a quaint outlandish fashion; some wore short doublets, others jerkins, with long knives in their belts, and most of them had enormous breeches, of similar style with that of the guide's. Their visages, too, were peculiar: one had a large beard, broad face, and small piggish eyes: the face of another seemed to consist entirely of nose, and was surmounted by a white sugarloaf hat, set off with a little red cock's tail. They all had beards, of various shapes and colors. There was one who seemed to be the commander. He was a stout old gentleman, with a weather-beaten countenance; he wore a laced doublet, broad belt and hanger, high crowned hat and feather, red stockings, and high-heeled shoes, with roses in them. The whole group reminded Rip of the figures in an old Flemish painting, in the parlor of Dominie Van Shaick, the village parson, and which had been brought over from Holland at the time of the settlement.

What seemed particularly odd to Rip was, that though these folks were evidently amusing themselves, yet they maintained the gravest faces, the most mysterious silence, and were, withal, the most melancholy party of pleasure he had ever witnessed. Nothing interrupted the stillness of the scene but the noise of the balls, which, whenever they were rolled, echoed along the mountains like rumbling peals of thunder.

As Rip and his companion approached them, they suddenly desisted from their play, and stared at him with such fixed statue-like gaze, and such strange, uncouth, lack-lustre countenances, that his heart turned within him, and his knees smote together. His companion now emptied the contents of the keg into large flagons, and made signs to him to wait upon the company. He obeyed with fear and trembling; they quaffed the liquor in profound silence, and then returned to their game.

By degrees Rip's awe and apprehension subsided. He even ventured, when no eye was fixed upon him, to taste the beverage, which he found had much of the flavor of excellent Hollands. He was naturally a thirsty soul, and was soon tempted to repeat the draught. One taste provoked another; and he reiterated his visits to the flagon so often that at length his senses were overpowered, his eyes swam in his head, his head gradually declined, and he fell into a deep sleep.

On waking, he found himself on the green knoll whence he had first seen the old man of the glen. He rubbed his eyes—it was a bright sunny morning. The birds were hopping and twittering among the bushes, and the eagle was wheeling aloft, and breasting the pure mountain breeze. "Surely," thought Rip, "I have not slept here all night." He recalled the occurrences before he fell asleep. The strange man with a keg of liquor—the mountain ravine—the wild retreat among the rocks—the wobegone party at nine-pins—the flagon—"Oh! that flagon! that wicked flagon!" thought Rip—"what excuse shall I make to Dame Van Winkle!"

He looked round for his gun, but in place of the clean well-oiled fowling-piece, he found an old firelock lying by him, the barrel incrusted with rust, the lock falling off, and the stock worm-eaten. He now suspected that the grave roysterers of the mountain had put a trick upon him, and, having dosed him with liquor, had robbed him of his gun. Wolf, too, had disappeared, but he might have strayed away after a squirrel or partridge. He whistled after him and shouted his name, but all in vain; the echoes repeated his whistle and shout, but no dog was to be seen.

He determined to revisit the scene of the last evening's gambol, and if he met with any of the party, to demand his dog and gun. As he rose to walk, he found himself stiff in the joints, and wanting in his usual activity. "These mountain beds do not agree with me," thought Rip, "and if this frolic should lay me up with a fit of the rheumatism, I shall have a blessed time with Dame Van Winkle." With some difficulty he got down into the glen: he found the gully up which he and his companion had ascended the preceding evening; but to his astonishment a mountain stream was now foaming down it, leaping from rock to rock, and filling the glen with babbling murmurs. He, however, made shift to scramble up its sides, working his toilsome way through thickets of birch, sassafras, and witch-hazel, and sometimes tripped up or entangled by the wild grapevines that twisted their coils or tendrils from tree to tree, and spread a kind of network in his path.

At length he reached to where the ravine had opened through the cliffs to the amphitheatre; but no traces of such opening remained. The rocks presented a high impenetrable wall over which the torrent came tumbling in a sheet of feathery foam, and fell into a broad deep basin, black from the shadows of the surrounding forest. Here, then, poor Rip was brought to a stand. He again called and whistled after his dog; he was only answered by the cawing of a flock of idle crows, sporting high in air about a dry tree that overhung a sunny precipice; and who, secure in their elevation, seemed to look down and scoff at the poor man's perplexities. What was to be done? the morning was passing away, and Rip felt famished for want of his breakfast. He grieved to give up his dog and gun; he dreaded to meet his wife; but it would not do to starve among the mountains. He shook his head, shouldered the rusty firelock, and, with a heart full of trouble and anxiety, turned his steps homeward.

As he approached the village he met a number of people, but none whom he knew, which somewhat surprised him, for he had thought himself acquainted with every one in the country round. Their dress, too, was of a different fashion from that to which he was accustomed. They all stared at him with equal marks of surprise, and whenever they cast their eyes upon him, invariably stroked their chins. The constant recurrence of this gesture induced Rip, involuntarily, to do the same, when, to his astonishment, he found his beard had grown a foot long!

He had now entered the skirts of the village. A troop of strange children ran at his heels, hooting after him, and pointing at his gray beard. The dogs, too, not one of which he recognized for an old acquaintance, barked at him as he passed. The very village was altered; it was larger and more populous. There were rows of houses which he had never seen before, and those which had been his familiar haunts had disappeared. Strange names were over the doors—strange faces at the windows—every thing was strange. His mind now misgave him; he began to doubt whether both he and the world around him were not bewitched. Surely this was his native village, which he had left but the day before. There stood the Kaatskill mountains—there ran the silver Hudson at a distance—there was every hill and dale precisely as it had always been—Rip was sorely perplexed—"That flagon last night," thought he, "has addled my poor head sadly!"

It was with some difficulty that he found the way to his own house, which he approached with silent awe, expecting every moment to hear the shrill voice of Dame Van Winkle. He found the house gone to decay—the roof fallen in, the windows shattered, and the doors off the hinges. A half-starved dog that looked like Wolf was skulking about it. Rip called him by name, but the cur snarled, showed his teeth, and passed on. This was an unkind cut indeed—"My very dog," sighed poor Rip, "has forgotten me!"

He entered the house, which, to tell the truth, Dame Van Winkle had always kept in neat order. It was empty, forlorn, and apparently abandoned. This desolateness overcame all his connubial fears—he called loudly for his wife and children—the lonely chambers rang for a moment with his voice, and then all again was silence.

He now hurried forth, and hastened to his old resort, the village inn—but it too was gone. A large rickety wooden building stood in its place, with great gaping windows, some of them broken and mended with old hats and petticoats, and over the door was painted, "The Union Hotel, by Jonathan Doolittle." Instead of the great tree that used to shelter the quiet little Dutch inn of yore, there now was reared a tall naked pole, with something on the top that looked like a red night-cap, and from it was fluttering a flag, on which was a singular assemblage of stars and stripes—all this was strange and incomprehensible. He recognized on the sign, however, the ruby face of King George, under which he had smoked so many a peaceful pipe; but even this was singularly metamorphosed. The red coat was changed for one of blue and buff, a sword was held in the hand instead of a sceptre, the head was decorated with a cocked hat, and underneath was painted in large characters, GENERAL WASHINGTON.

There was, as usual, a crowd of folk about the door, but none that Rip recollected. The very character of the people seemed changed. There was a busy, bustling, disputatious tone about it, instead of the accustomed phlegm and drowsy tranquillity. He looked in vain for the sage Nicholas Vedder, with his broad face, double chin, and fair long pipe, uttering clouds of tobacco-smoke instead of idle speeches; or Van Bummel, the schoolmaster, doling forth the contents of an ancient newspaper. In place of these, a lean, bilious-looking fellow, with his pockets full of handbills, was haranguing vehemently about rights of citizens—elections—members of congress—liberty—Bunker's Hill—heroes of seventy-six—and other words, which were a perfect Babylonish jargon to the bewildered Van Winkle.

The appearance of Rip, with his long grizzled beard, his rusty fowling-piece, his uncouth dress, and an army of women and children at his heels, soon attracted the attention of the tavern politicians. They crowded round him, eyeing him from head to foot with great curiosity. The orator bustled up to him, and, drawing him partly aside, inquired "on which side he voted?" Rip stared in vacant stupidity. Another short but busy little fellow pulled him by the arm, and, rising on tiptoe, inquired in his ear, "Whether he was Federal or Democrat?" Rip was equally at a loss to comprehend the question; when a knowing, self-important old gentleman, in a sharp cocked hat, made his way through the crowd, putting them to the right and left with his elbows as he passed, and planting himself before Van Winkle, with one arm akimbo, the other resting on his cane, his keen eyes and sharp hat penetrating, as it were, into his very soul, demanded in an austere tone, "what brought him to the election with a gun on his shoulder, and a mob at his heels, and whether he meant to breed a riot in the village?"—"Alas! gentlemen," cried Rip, somewhat dismayed, "I am a poor quiet man, a native of the place, and a loyal subject of the king, God bless him!"

Here a general shout burst from the bystanders—"A tory! a tory! a spy! a refugee! hustle him! away with him!" It was with great difficulty that the self-important man in the cocked hat restored order; and, having assumed a ten-fold austerity of brow, demanded again of the unknown culprit, what he came there for, and whom he was seeking? The poor man humbly assured him that he meant no harm, but merely came there in search of some of his neighbors, who used to keep about the tavern.

"Well—who are they?—name them."

Rip bethought himself a moment, and inquired, "Where's Nicholas Vedder?"

There was a silence for a little while, when an old man replied, in a thin piping voice, "Nicholas Vedder! swhy, he is dead and gone these eighteen years! There was a wooden tombstone in the church-yard that used to tell all about him, but that's rotten and gone too."

"Where's Brom Dutcher?"

"Oh, he went off to the army in the beginning of the war; some say he was killed at the storming of Stony Point—others say he was drowned in a squall at the foot of Antony's Nose. I don't know—he never came back again."

"Where's Van Bummel, the schoolmaster?"

"He went off to the wars too, was a great militia general, and is now in congress."

Rip's heart died away at hearing of these sad changes in his home and friends, and finding himself thus alone in the world. Every answer puzzled him too, by treating of such enormous lapses of time, and of matters which he could not understand: war—congress—Stony Point;—he had no courage to ask after any more friends, but cried out in despair, "Does nobody here know Rip Van Winkle?"

"Oh, Rip Van Winkle!" exclaimed two or three, "Oh, to be sure! that's Rip Van Winkle yonder, leaning against the tree."

Rip looked, and beheld a precise counterpart of himself, as he went up the mountain: apparently as lazy, and certainly as ragged. The poor fellow was now completely confounded. He doubted his own identity, and whether he was himself or another man. In the midst of his bewilderment, the man in the cocked hat demanded who he was, and what was his name?

"God knows," exclaimed he, at his wit's end; "I'm not myself—I'm somebody else—that's me yonder—no—that's somebody else got into my shoes—I was myself last night, but I fell asleep on the mountain, and they've changed my gun, and every thing's changed, and I'm changed, and I can't tell what's my name, or who I am!"

The bystanders began now to look at each other, nod, wink significantly, and tap their fingers against their foreheads. There was a whisper, also, about securing the gun, and keeping the old fellow from doing mischief, at the very suggestion of which the self-important man in the cocked hat retired with some precipitation. At this critical moment a fresh comely woman pressed through the throng to get a peep at the gray-bearded man. She had a chubby child in her arms, which, frightened at his looks, began to cry. "Hush, Rip," cried she, "hush, you little fool; the old man won't hurt you." The name of the child, the air of the mother, the tone of her voice, all awakened a train of recollections in his mind. "What is your name, my good woman?" asked he.

"Judith Gardenier."

"And your father's name?"

"Ah, poor man, Rip Van Winkle was his name, but it's twenty years since he went away from home with his gun, and never has been heard of since—his dog came home without him; but whether he shot himself, or was carried away by the Indians, nobody can tell. I was then but a little girl."

Rip had but one question more to ask; but he put it with a faltering voice:

"Where's your mother?"

"Oh, she too had died but a short time since; she broke a blood-vessel in a fit of passion at a New-England peddler."

There was a drop of comfort, at least, in this intelligence. The honest man could contain himself no longer. He caught his daughter and her child in his arms. "I am your father!" cried he "Young Rip Van Winkle once—old Rip Van Winkle now!—Does nobody know poor Rip Van Winkle?"

All stood amazed, until an old woman, tottering out from among the crowd, put her hand to her brow, and peering under it in his face for a moment, exclaimed, "Sure enough! it is Rip Van Winkle—it is himself! Welcome home again, old neighbor—Why, where have you been these twenty long years?"

Rip's story was soon told, for the whole twenty years had been to him but as one night. The neighbors stared when they heard it; some were seen to wink at each other, and put their tongues in their cheeks: and the self-important man in the cocked hat, who, when the alarm was over, had returned to the field, screwed down the corners of his mouth, and shook his head—upon which there was a general shaking of the head throughout the assemblage.

It was determined, however, to take the opinion of old Peter Vanderdonk, who was seen slowly advancing up the road. He was a descendant of the historian of that name, who wrote one of the earliest accounts of the province. Peter was the most ancient inhabitant of the village, and well versed in all the wonderful events and traditions of the neighborhood. He recollected Rip at once, and corroborated his story in the most satisfactory manner. He assured the company that it was a fact, handed down from his ancestor the historian, that the Kaatskill mountains had always been haunted by strange beings. That it was affirmed that the great Hendrick Hudson, the first discoverer of the river and country, kept a kind of vigil there every twenty years, with his crew of the Half-moon; being permitted in this way to revisit the scenes of his enterprise, and keep a guardian eye upon the river, and the great city called by his name. That his father had once seen them in their old Dutch dresses playing at nine-pins in a hollow of the mountain; and that he himself had heard, one summer afternoon, the sound of their balls, like distant peals of thunder.

To make a long story short, the company broke up, and returned to the more important concerns of the election. Rip's daughter took him home to live with her; she had a snug, well-furnished house, and a stout cheery farmer for a husband, whom Rip recollected for one of the urchins that used to climb upon his back. As to Rip's son and heir, who was the ditto of himself, seen leaning against the tree, he was employed to work on the farm; but evinced an hereditary disposition to attend to any thing else but his business.

Rip now resumed his old walks and habits; he soon found many of his former cronies, though all rather the worse for the wear and tear of time; and preferred making friends among the rising generation, with whom he soon grew into great favor.

Having nothing to do at home, and being arrived at that happy age when a man can be idle with impunity, he took his place once more on the bench at the inn door, and was reverenced as one of the patriarchs of the village, and a chronicle of the old times "before the war." It was some time before he could get into the regular track of gossip, or could be made to comprehend the strange events that had taken place during his torpor. How that there had been a revolutionary war—that the country had thrown off the yoke of old England—and that, instead of being a subject of his Majesty George the Third, he was now a free citizen of the United States. Rip, in fact, was no politician; the changes of states and empires made but little impression on him; but there was one species of despotism under which he had long groaned, and that was—petticoat government. Happily that was at an end; he had got his neck out of the yoke of matrimony, and could go in and out whenever he pleased, without dreading the tyranny of Dame Van Winkle. Whenever her name was mentioned, however, he shook his head, shrugged his shoulders, and cast up his eyes; which might pass either for an expression of resignation to his fate, or joy at his deliverance.

He used to tell his story to every stranger that arrived at Mr. Doolittle's hotel. He was observed, at first, to vary on some points every time he told it, which was, doubtless, owing to his having so recently awaked. It at last settled down precisely to the tale I have related, and not a man, woman, or child in the neighborhood, but knew it by heart. Some always pretended to doubt the reality of it, and insisted that Rip had been out of his head, and that this was one point on which he always remained flighty. The old Dutch inhabitants, however, almost universally gave it full credit. Even to this day they never hear a thunder-storm of a summer afternoon about the Kaatskill, but they say Hendrick Hudson and his crew are at their game of nine-pins; and it is a common wish of all hen-pecked husbands in the neighborhood, when life hangs heavy on their hands, that they might have a quieting draught out of Rip Van Winkle's flagon.

*   *   *   *   *   *   *   *

The foregoing Tale, one would suspect, had been suggested to Mr. Knickerbocker by a little German superstition about the Emperor Frederick der Rothbart, and the Kyffhauser mountain: the subjoined note, however, which he had appended to the tale, shows that it is an absolute fact, narrated with his usual fidelity:

"The story of Rip Van Winkle may seem incredible to many, but nevertheless I give it my full belief, for I know the vicinity of our old Dutch settlements to have been very subject to marvellous events and appearances. Indeed, I have heard many stranger stories than this, in the villages along the Hudson; all of which were too well authenticated to admit of a doubt. I have even talked with Rip Van Winkle myself, who, when last I saw him, was a very venerable old man, and so perfectly rational and consistent on every other point, that I think no conscientious person could refuse to take this into the bargain; nay, I have seen a certificate on the subject taken before a country justice and signed with a cross, in the justice's own handwriting. The story, therefore, is beyond the possibility of doubt.—D. K."

*   *   *   *   *   *   *   *

Postscript

The following are travelling notes from a memorandum-book of Mr. Knickerbocker:

The Kaatsberg, or Catskill Mountains, have always been a region full of fable. The Indians considered them the abode of spirits, who influenced the weather, spreading sunshine or clouds over the landscape, and sending good or bad hunting seasons. They were ruled by an old squaw spirit, said to be their mother. She dwelt on the highest peak of the Catskills, and had charge of the doors of day and night to open and shut them at the proper hour. She hung up the new moons in the skies, and cut up the old ones into stars. In times of drought, if properly propitiated, she would spin light summer clouds out of cobwebs and morning dew, and send them off from the crest of the mountain, flake after flake, like flakes of carded cotton, to float in the air; until, dissolved by the heat of the sun, they would fall in gentle showers, causing the grass to spring, the fruits to ripen, and the corn to grow an inch an hour. If displeased, however, she would brew up clouds black as ink, sitting in the midst of them like a bottle-bellied spider in the midst of its web; and when these clouds broke, wo betide the valleys!

In old times, say the Indian traditions, there was a kind of Manitou or Spirit, who kept about the wildest recesses of the Catskill Mountains, and took a mischievous pleasure in wreaking all kinds of evils and vexations upon the red men. Sometimes he would assume the form of a bear, a panther, or a deer, lead the bewildered hunter a weary chase through tangled forests and among ragged rocks; and then spring off with a loud ho! ho! leaving him aghast on the brink of a beetling precipice or raging torrent.

The favorite abode of this Manitou is still shown. It is a great rock or cliff on the loneliest part of the mountains, and, from the flowering vines which clamber about it, and the wild flowers which abound in its neighborhood, is known by the name of Garden Rock. Near the foot of it is a small lake, the haunt of the solitary bittern, with water-snakes basking in the sun on the leaves of the pond-lilies which lie on the surface. This place was held in great awe by the Indians, insomuch that the boldest hunter would not pursue his game within its precincts. Once upon a time, however, a hunter who had lost his way, penetrated to the garden rock, where he beheld a number of gourds placed in the crotches of trees. One of these he seized and made off with it, but in the hurry of his retreat he let it fall among the rocks, when a great stream gushed forth, which washed him away and swept him down precipices, where he was dashed to pieces, and the stream made its way to the Hudson, and continues to flow to the present day; being the identical stream known by the name of the Kaaters-kill.

The Spectre Bridegroom
A Traveller's Tale*

He that supper for is dight,
He lyes full cold, I trow, this night!
Yestreen to chamber I him led,
This night Gray-Steel has made his bed.
Sir Eger, Sir Grahame, and Sir Gray-Steel

ON THE summit of one of the heights of the Odenwald, a wild and romantic tract of Upper Germany, that lies not far from the confluence of the Main and the Rhine, there stood, many, many years since, the Castle of the Baron Von Landshort. It is now quite fallen to decay, and almost buried among beech trees and dark firs; about which, however, its old watch-tower may still be seen, struggling, like the former possessor I have mentioned, to carry a high head, and look down upon the neighboring country.

The baron was a dry branch of the great family of Katzenellenbogen,[1] and inherited the relics of the property, and all the pride of his ancestors. Though the warlike disposition of his predecessors had much impaired the family possessions, yet the baron still endeavored to keep up some show of former state. The times were peaceable, and the German nobles, in general,

* The erudite reader, well versed in good-for-nothing lore, will perceive that the above tale must have been suggested to the old Swiss by a little French anecdote, a circumstance said to have taken place at Paris.

[1] i. e., Cat's-elbow. The name of a family of those parts very powerful in former times. The appellation, we are told, was given in compliment to a peerless dame of the family, celebrated for her fine arm.

had abandoned their inconvenient old castles, perched like eagles' nests among the mountains, and had built more convenient residences in the valleys: still the baron remained proudly drawn up in his little fortress, cherishing, with hereditary inveteracy, all the old family feuds; so that he was on ill terms with some of his nearest neighbors, on account of disputes that had happened between their great-great-grandfathers.

The baron had but one child, a daughter; but nature, when she grants but one child, always compensates by making it a prodigy; and so it was with the daughter of the baron. All the nurses, gossips, and country cousins, assured her father that she had not her equal for beauty in all Germany; and who should know better than they? She had, moreover, been brought up with great care under the superintendence of two maiden aunts, who had spent some years of their early life at one of the little German courts, and were skilled in all the branches of knowledge necessary to the education of a fine lady. Under their instructions she became a miracle of accomplishments. By the time she was eighteen, she could embroider to admiration, and had worked whole histories of the saints in tapestry, with such strength of expression in their countenances, that they looked like so many souls in purgatory. She could read without great difficulty, and had spelled her way through several church legends, and almost all the chivalric wonders of the Heldenbuch. She had even made considerable proficiency in writing; could sign her own name without missing a letter, and so legibly, that her aunts could read it without spectacles. She excelled in making little elegant good-for-nothing lady-like nicknacks of all kinds; was versed in the most abstruse dancing of the day; played a number of airs on the harp and guitar; and knew all the tender ballads of the Minne-lieder by heart.

Her aunts, too, having been great flirts and coquettes in their younger days, were admirably calculated to be vigilant guardians and strict censors of the conduct of their niece; for there is no duenna so rigidly prudent, and inexorably decorous, as a superannuated coquette. She was rarely suffered out of their sight; never went beyond the domains of the castle, unless well attended, or rather well watched; had continual lectures read to her about strict decorum and implicit obedience; and, as to the men—pah!—she was taught to hold them at such a distance, and in such absolute distrust, that, unless properly authorized, she would not have cast a glance upon the handsomest cavalier in the world—no, not if he were even dying at her feet.

The good effects of this system were wonderfully apparent. The young lady was a pattern of docility and correctness. While others were wasting their sweetness in the glare of the world, and liable to be plucked and thrown aside by every hand, she was coyly blooming into fresh and lovely womanhood under the protection of those immaculate spinsters, like a rose-bud blushing forth among guardian thorns. Her aunts looked upon her with pride and exultation, and vaunted that though all the other young ladies in the world might go astray, yet, thank Heaven, nothing of the kind could happen to the heiress of Katzenellenbogen.

But, however scantily the Baron Von Landshort might be provided with children, his household was by no means a small one; for Providence had enriched him with abundance of poor relations. They, one and all, possessed the affectionate disposition common to humble relatives; were wonderfully attached to the baron, and took every possible occasion to come in swarms and enliven the castle. All family festivals were commemorated by these good people at the baron's expense; and when they were filled with good cheer, they would declare that there was nothing on earth so delightful as these family meetings, these jubilees of the heart.

The baron, though a small man, had a large soul, and it

swelled with satisfaction at the consciousness of being the greatest man in the little world about him. He loved to tell long stories about the dark old warriors whose portraits looked grimly down from the walls around, and he found no listeners equal to those who fed at his expense. He was much given to the marvellous, and a firm believer in all those supernatural tales with which every mountain and valley in Germany abounds. The faith of his guests exceeded even his own: they listened to every tale of wonder with open eyes and mouth, and never failed to be astonished, even though repeated for the hundredth time. Thus lived the Baron Von Landshort, the oracle of his table, the absolute monarch of his little territory, and happy, above all things, in the persuasion that he was the wisest man of the age.

At the time of which my story treats, there was a great family gathering at the castle, on an affair of the utmost importance: it was to receive the destined bridegroom of the baron's daughter. A negotiation had been carried on between the father and an old nobleman of Bavaria, to unite the dignity of their houses by the marriage of their children. The preliminaries had been conducted with proper punctilio. The young people were betrothed without seeing each other; and the time was appointed for the marriage ceremony. The young Count Von Altenburg had been recalled from the army for the purpose, and was actually on his way to the baron's to receive his bride. Missives had even been received from him, from Wurtzburg, where he was accidentally detained, mentioning the day and hour when he might be expected to arrive.

The castle was in a tumult of preparation to give him a suitable welcome. The fair bride had been decked out with uncommon care. The two aunts had superintended her toilet, and quarrelled the whole morning about every article of her dress. The young lady had taken advantage of their contest to follow the bent of her own taste; and fortunately it was a good one. She looked as lovely as youthful bridegroom could desire; and the flutter of expectation heightened the lustre of her charms.

The suffusions that mantled her face and neck, the gentle heaving of the bosom, the eye now and then lost in reverie, all betrayed the soft tumult that was going on in her little heart. The aunts were continually hovering around her; for maiden aunts are apt to take great interest in affairs of this nature. They were giving her a world of staid counsel how to deport herself, what to say, and in what manner to receive the expected lover.

The baron was no less busied in preparations. He had, in truth, nothing exactly to do: but he was naturally a fuming bustling little man, and could not remain passive when all the world was in a hurry. He worried from top to bottom of the castle with an air of infinite anxiety; he continually called the servants from their work to exhort them to be diligent; and buzzed about every hall and chamber, as idly restless and importunate as a blue-bottle fly on a warm summer's day.

In the meantime the fatted calf had been killed; the forests had rung with the clamor of the huntsmen; the kitchen was crowded with good cheer; the cellars had yielded up whole oceans of Rhein-wein and Ferne-wein; and even the great Heidelberg tun had been laid under contribution. Every thing was ready to receive the distinguished guest with Saus und Braus in the true spirit of German hospitality—but the guest delayed to make his appearance. Hour rolled after hour. The sun, that had poured his downward rays upon the rich forest of the Odenwald, now just gleamed along the summits of the mountains. The baron mounted the highest tower, and strained his eyes in hope of catching a distant sight of the count and his attendants. Once he thought he beheld them; the sound of horns came floating from the valley, prolonged by the mountain echoes. A number of horsemen were seen far below, slowly advancing along the road; but when they had nearly reached the foot of the mountain, they suddenly struck off in a different direction. The last ray of sunshine departed—the bats began to flit by in the twilight—the road grew dimmer and dimmer to the view; and nothing appeared stirring in it but now and then a peasant lagging homeward from his labor.

While the old castle of Landshort was in this state of perplexity, a very interesting scene was transacting in a different part of the Odenwald.

The young Count Von Altenburg was tranquilly pursuing his route in that sober jog-trot way, in which a man travels toward matrimony when his friends have taken all the trouble and uncertainty of courtship off his hands, and a bride is waiting for him, as certainly as a dinner at the end of his journey. He had encountered at Wurtzburg, a youthful companion in arms, with whom he had seen some service on the frontiers; Herman Von Starkenfaust, one of the stoutest hands, and worthiest hearts, of German chivalry, who was now returning from the army. His father's castle was not far distant from the old fortress of Landshort, although an hereditary feud rendered the families hostile, and strangers to each other.

In the warm-hearted moment of recognition, the young friends related all their past adventures and fortunes, and the count gave the whole history of his intended nuptials with a young lady whom he had never seen, but of whose charms he had received the most enrapturing descriptions.

As the route of the friends lay in the same direction, they agreed to perform the rest of their journey together; and, that they might do it the more leisurely, set off from Wurtzburg at an early hour, the count having given directions for his retinue to follow and overtake him.

They beguiled their wayfaring with recollections of their military scenes and adventures; but the count was apt to be a little tedious, now and then, about the reputed charms of his bride, and the felicity that awaited him.

In this way they had entered among the mountains of the Odenwald, and were traversing one of its most lonely and thickly-wooded passes. It is well known that the forests of Germany have always been as much infested by robbers as its castles by spectres; and, at this time, the former were particularly numerous, from the hordes of disbanded soldiers wandering about the country. It will not appear extraordinary, therefore, that the cavaliers were attacked by a gang of these stragglers, in the midst of the forest. They defended themselves with bravery, but were nearly overpowered, when the count's retinue arrived to their assistance. At sight of them the robbers fled, but not until the count had received a mortal wound. He was slowly and carefully conveyed back to the city of Wurtzburg, and a friar summoned from a neighboring convent, who was famous for his skill in administering to both soul and body; but half of his skill was superfluous; the moments of the unfortunate count were numbered.

With his dying breath he entreated his friend to repair instantly to the castle of Landshort, and explain the fatal cause of his not keeping his appointment with his bride. Though not the most ardent of lovers, he was one of the most punctilious of men, and appeared earnestly solicitous that his mission should be speedily and courteously executed. "Unless this is done," said he, "I shall not sleep quietly in my grave!" He repeated these last words with peculiar solemnity. A request, at a moment so impressive, admitted no hesitation. Starkenfaust endeavored to soothe him to calmness; promised faithfully to execute his wish, and gave him his hand in solemn pledge. The dying man pressed it in acknowledgment, but soon lapsed into delirium—raved about his bride—his engagements—his plighted word; ordered his horse, that he might ride to the castle of Landshort; and expired in the fancied act of vaulting into the saddle.

Starkenfaust bestowed a sigh and a soldier's tear on the untimely fate of his comrade; and then pondered on the awkward mission he had undertaken. His heart was heavy, and his head perplexed; for he was to present himself an unbidden guest among hostile people, and to damp their festivity with tidings fatal to their hopes. Still there were certain whisperings of curiosity in his bosom to see this far-famed beauty of Katzenellenbogen, so cautiously shut up from the world; for he was a passionate admirer of the sex, and there was a dash of eccentricity and enterprise in his character that made him fond of all singular adventure.

Previous to his departure he made all due arrangements with the holy fraternity of the convent for the funeral solemnities of his friend, who was to be buried in the cathedral of Wurtzburg, near some of his illustrious relatives; and the mourning retinue of the count took charge of his remains.

It is now high time that we should return to the ancient family of Katzenellenbogen, who were impatient for their guest, and still more for their dinner; and to the worthy little baron, whom we left airing himself on the watchtower.

Night closed in, but still no guest arrived. The baron descended from the tower in despair. The banquet, which had been delayed from hour to hour, could no longer be postponed. The meats were already overdone; the cook in an agony; and the whole household had the look of a garrison that had been reduced by famine. The baron was obliged reluctantly to give orders for the feast without the presence of the guest. All were seated at table, and just on the point of commencing, when the sound of a horn from without the gate gave notice of the approach of a stranger. Another long blast filled the old courts of the castle with its echoes, and was answered by the warder from the walls. The baron hastened to receive his future son-in-law.

The drawbridge had been let down, and the stranger was before the gate. He was a tall, gallant cavalier, mounted on a black steed. His countenance was pale, but he had a beaming, romantic eye, and an air of stately melancholy. The baron was a little mortified that he should have come in this simple, solitary style. His dignity for a moment was ruffled, and he felt disposed to consider it a want of proper respect for the important occasion, and the important family with which he was to be connected. He pacified himself, however, with the conclusion, that it must have been youthful impatience which had induced him thus to spur on sooner than his attendants.

"I am sorry," said the stranger, "to break in upon you thus unseasonably—"

Here the baron interrupted him with a world of compliments and greetings; for, to tell the truth, he prided himself upon his courtesy and eloquence. The stranger attempted, once or twice, to stem the torrent of words, but in vain, so he bowed his head and suffered it to flow on. By the time the baron had come to a pause, they had reached the inner court of the castle; and the stranger was again about to speak, when he was once more interrupted by the appearance of the female part of the family, leading forth the shrinking and blushing bride. He gazed on her for a moment as one entranced; it seemed as if his whole soul beamed forth in the gaze, and rested upon that lovely form. One of the maiden aunts whispered something in her ear; she made an effort to speak; her moist blue eye was timidly raised; gave a shy glance of inquiry on the stranger; and was cast again to the ground. The words died away; but there was a sweet smile playing about her lips, and a soft dimpling of the cheek that showed her glance had not been unsatisfactory. It was impossible for a girl of the fond age of eighteen, highly predisposed for love and matrimony, not to be pleased with so gallant a cavalier.

The late hour at which the guest had arrived left no time for parley. The baron was peremptory, and deferred all particular conversation until the morning, and led the way to the untasted banquet.

It was served up in the great hall of the castle. Around the walls hung the hard-favored portraits of the heroes of the house of Katzenellenbogen, and the trophies which they had gained in the field and in the chase. Hacked corslets, splintered jousting spears, and tattered banners, were mingled with the spoils of sylvan warfare; the jaws of the wolf, and the tusks of the boar, grinned horribly among cross-bows and battle-axes, and a huge pair of antlers branched immediately over the head of the youthful bridegroom.

The cavalier took but little notice of the company or the entertainment. He scarcely tasted the banquet, but seemed absorbed in admiration of his bride. He conversed in a low tone that could not be overheard—for the language of love is never loud; but where is the female ear so dull that it cannot catch the softest whisper of the lover? There was a mingled tenderness and gravity in his manner, that appeared to have a powerful effect upon the young lady. Her color came and went as she listened with deep attention. Now and then she made some blushing reply, and when his eye was turned away, she would steal a sidelong glance at his romantic countenance, and heave a gentle sigh of tender happiness. It was evident that the young couple were completely enamored. The aunts, who were deeply versed in the mysteries of the heart, declared that they had fallen in love with each other at first sight.

The feast went on merrily, or at least noisily, for the guests were all blessed with those keen appetites that attend upon light purses and mountain air. The baron told his best and longest stories, and never had he told them so well, or with such great effect. If there was any thing marvellous, his auditors were lost in astonishment; and if any thing facetious, they were sure to laugh exactly in the right place. The baron, it is true, like most great men, was too dignified to utter any joke but a dull one; it was always enforced, however, by a bumper of excellent Hochheimer; and even a dull joke, at one's own table, served up with jolly old wine, is irresistible. Many good things were said by poorer and keener wits, that would not bear repeating except on similar occasions; many sly speeches whispered in ladies' ears, that almost convulsed them with suppressed laughter; and a song or two roared out by a poor, but merry and broad-faced cousin of the baron, that absolutely made the maiden aunts hold up their fans.

Amidst all this revelry, the stranger guest maintained a most singular and unseasonable gravity. His countenance assumed a deeper cast of dejection as the evening advanced; and, strange as it may appear, even the baron's jokes seemed only to render him the more melancholy. At times he was lost in thought, and at times there was a perturbed and restless wandering of the eye that bespoke a mind but ill at ease. His conversations with the bride became more and more earnest and mysterious. Lowering clouds began to steal over the fair serenity of her brow, and tremors to run through her tender frame.

All this could not escape the notice of the company. Their gayety was chilled by the unaccountable gloom of the bridegroom; their spirits were infected; whispers and glances were interchanged, accompanied by shrugs and dubious shakes of the head. The song and the laugh grew less and less frequent; there were dreary pauses in the conversation, which were at length succeeded by wild tales and supernatural legends. One dismal story produced another still more dismal, and the baron nearly frightened some of the ladies into hysterics with the history of the goblin horseman that carried away the fair

Leonora; a dreadful story, which has since been put into excellent verse, and is read and believed by all the world.

The bridegroom listened to this tale with profound attention. He kept his eyes steadily fixed on the baron, and, as the story drew to a close, began gradually to rise from his seat, growing taller and taller, until, in the baron's entranced eye, he seemed almost to tower into a giant. The moment the tale was finished, he heaved a deep sigh, and took a solemn farewell of the company. They were all amazement. The baron was perfectly thunderstruck.

"What! going to leave the castle at midnight? why, every thing was prepared for his reception; a chamber was ready for him if he wished to retire."

The stranger shook his head mournfully and mysteriously; "I must lay my head in a different chamber to-night!"

There was something in this reply, and the tone in which it was uttered, that made the baron's heart misgive him; but he rallied his forces, and repeated his hospitable entreaties.

The stranger shook his head silently, but positively, at every offer, and, waving his farewell to the company, stalked slowly out of the hall. The maiden aunts were absolutely petrified—the bride hung her head, and a tear stole to her eye.

The baron followed the stranger to the great court of the castle, where the black charger stood pawing the earth, and snorting with impatience.—When they had reached the portal, whose deep archway was dimly lighted by a cresset, the stranger paused, and addressed the baron in a hollow tone of voice, which the vaulted roof rendered still more sepulchral.

"Now that we are alone," said he, "I will impart to you the reason of my going. I have a solemn, and indispensable engagement—"

"Why," said the baron, "cannot you send some one in your place?"

"It admits of no substitute—I must attend it in person—I must away to Wurtzburg cathedral—"

"Ay," said the baron, plucking up spirit, "but not until to-morrow—to-morrow you shall take your bride there."

"No! no!" replied the stranger, with tenfold solemnity, "my engagement is with no bride—the worms! the worms expect me! I am a dead man—I have been slain by robbers—my body lies at Wurtzburg—at midnight I am to be buried—the grave is waiting for me—I must keep my appointment!"

He sprang on his black charger, dashed over the drawbridge, and the clattering of his horse's hoofs was lost in the whistling of the night blast.

The baron returned to the hall in the utmost consternation, and related what had passed. Two ladies fainted outright, others sickened at the idea of having banqueted with a spectre. It was the opinion of some, that this might be the wild huntsman, famous in German legend. Some talked of mountain sprites, of wood-demons, and of other supernatural beings, with which the good people of Germany have been so grievously harassed since time immemorial. One of the poor relations ventured to suggest that it might be some sportive evasion of the young cavalier, and that the very gloominess of the caprice seemed to accord with so melancholy a personage. This, however, drew on him the indignation of the whole company, and especially of the baron, who looked upon him as little better than an infidel; so that he was fain to abjure his heresy as speedily as possible, and come into the faith of the true believers.

But whatever may have been the doubts entertained, they were completely put to an end by the arrival, next day, of regular missives, confirming the intelligence of the young count's murder, and his interment in Wurtzburg cathedral.

The dismay at the castle may well be imagined. The baron shut himself up in his chamber. The guests, who had come to rejoice with him, could not think of abandoning him in his distress. They wandered about the courts, or collected in groups in the hall, shaking their heads and shrugging their shoulders, at the troubles of so good a man; and sat longer than ever at table, and ate and drank more stoutly than ever, by way of keeping up their spirits. But the situation of the widowed bride was the most pitiable. To have lost a husband before she had even embraced him—and such a husband! if the very spectre could be so gracious and noble, what must have been the living man. She filled the house with lamentations.

On the night of the second day of her widowhood, she had retired to her chamber, accompanied by one of her aunts, who insisted on sleeping with her. The aunt, who was one of the best tellers of ghost stories in all Germany, had just been recounting one of her longest, and had fallen asleep in the very midst of it. The chamber was remote, and overlooked a small garden. The niece lay pensively gazing at the beams of the rising moon, as they trembled on the leaves of an aspen-tree before the lattice. The castle clock had just tolled midnight, when a soft strain of music stole up from the garden. She rose hastily from her bed, and stepped lightly to the window. A tall figure stood among the shadows of the trees. As it raised its head, a beam of moonlight fell upon the countenance. Heaven and earth! she beheld the Spectre Bridegroom! A loud shriek at that moment burst upon her ear, and her aunt, who had been awakened by the music, and had followed her silently to the window, fell into her arms. When she looked again, the spectre had disappeared.

Of the two females, the aunt now required the most soothing, for she was perfectly beside herself with terror. As to the young lady, there was something, even in the spectre of her lover, that seemed endearing. There was still the semblance of manly beauty; and though the shadow of a man is but little calculated to satisfy the affections of a love-sick girl, yet, where the substance is not to be had, even that is consoling. The aunt declared she would never sleep in that chamber again; the niece, for once, was refractory, and declared as strongly that she would sleep in no other in the castle: the consequence was, that she had to sleep in it alone: but she drew a promise from her aunt not to relate the story of the spectre, lest she should be denied the only melancholy pleasure left her on earth—that of inhabiting the chamber over which the guardian shade of her lover kept its nightly vigils.

How long the good old lady would have observed this promise is uncertain, for she dearly loved to talk of the marvellous, and there is a triumph in being the first to tell a frightful story; it is, however, still quoted in the neighborhood, as a memorable instance of female secrecy, that she kept it to herself for a whole week; when she was suddenly absolved from all further restraint, by intelligence brought to the breakfast table one morning that the young lady was not to be found. Her room was empty—the bed had not been slept in—the window was open, and the bird had flown!

The astonishment and concern with which the intelligence was received, can only be imagined by those who have witnessed the agitation which the mishaps of a great man cause among his friends. Even the poor relations paused for a moment from the indefatigable labors of the trencher; when the aunt, who had at first been struck speechless, wrung her hands, and shrieked out, "The goblin! the goblin! she's carried away by the goblin."

In a few words she related the fearful scene of the garden, and concluded that the spectre must have carried off his bride. Two of the domestics corroborated the opinion, for they had heard the clattering of a horse's hoofs down the mountain about midnight, and had no doubt that it was the spectre on his black charger, bearing her away to the tomb. All present were struck with the direful probability; for events of the kind are extremely common in Germany, as many well authenticated histories bear witness.

What a lamentable situation was that of the poor baron! What a heart-rending dilemma for a fond father, and a member of the great family of Katzenellenbogen! His only daughter had either been rapt away to the grave, or he was to have some wood-demon for a son-in-law, and, perchance, a troop of goblin grandchildren. As usual, he was completely bewildered, and all the castle in an uproar. The men were ordered to take horse, and scour every road and path and glen of the Odenwald. The baron himself had just drawn on his jack-boots, girded on his sword, and was about to mount his steed to sally forth on the doubtful quest, when he was brought to a pause by a new apparition. A lady was seen approaching the castle, mounted on a palfrey, attended by a cavalier on horseback. She galloped up to the gate, sprang from her horse, and falling at the baron's feet, embraced his knees. It was his lost daughter, and her companion—the Spectre Bridegroom! The baron was astounded. He looked at his daughter, then at the spectre, and almost doubted the evidence of his senses. The latter, too, was wonderfully improved in his appearance since his visit to the world of spirits. His dress was splendid, and set off a noble figure of manly symmetry. He was no longer pale and melancholy. His fine countenance was flushed with the glow of youth, and joy rioted in his large dark eye.

The mystery was soon cleared up. The cavalier (for, in truth, as you must have known all the while, he was no goblin) announced himself as Sir Herman Von Starkenfaust. He related his adventure with the young count. He told how he had hastened to the castle to deliver the unwelcome tidings, but that the eloquence of the baron had interrupted him in every attempt to tell his tale. How the sight of the bride had completely captivated him, and that to pass a few hours near her, he had tacitly suffered the mistake to continue. How he had been sorely perplexed in what way to make a decent retreat, until the baron's goblin stories had suggested his eccentric exit. How, fearing the feudal hostility of the family, he had repeated his visits by stealth—had haunted the garden beneath the young lady's window—had wooed—had won—had borne away in triumph—and, in a word, had wedded the fair.

Under any other circumstances the baron would have been inflexible, for he was tenacious of paternal authority, and devoutly obstinate in all family feuds; but he loved his daughter; he had lamented her as lost; he rejoiced to find her still alive; and, though her husband was of a hostile house, yet, thank Heaven, he was not a goblin. There was something, it must be acknowledged, that did not exactly accord with his notions of strict veracity, in the joke the knight had passed upon him of his being a dead man; but several old friends present, who had served in the wars, assured him that every stratagem was excusable in love, and that the cavalier was entitled to especial privilege, having lately served as a trooper.

Matters, therefore, were happily arranged. The baron pardoned the young couple on the spot. The revels at the castle were resumed. The poor relations overwhelmed this new m ember of the family with loving kindness; he was so gallant, so generous—and so rich. The aunts, it is true, were somewhat scandalized that their system of strict seclusion, and passive obedience should be so badly exemplified, but attributed it all to their negligence in not having the windows grated. One of them was particularly mortified at having her marvellous story marred, and that the only spectre she had ever seen should turn out a counterfeit; but the niece seemed perfectly happy at having found him substantial flesh and blood—and so the story ends.

The Devil and Tom Walker

A FEW miles from Boston, in Massachusetts, there is a deep inlet winding several miles into the interior of the country from Charles Bay, and terminating in a thickly wooded swamp, or morass. On one side of this inlet is a beautiful dark grove; on the opposite side the land rises abruptly from the water's edge, into a high ridge on which grow a few scattered oaks of great age and immense size. Under one of these gigantic trees, according to old stories, there was a great amount of treasure buried by Kidd the pirate. The inlet allowed a facility to bring the money in a boat secretly and at night to the very foot of the hill. The elevation of the place permitted a good look out to be kept that no one was at hand, while the remarkable trees formed good landmarks by which the place might easily be found again. The old stories add, moreover, that the devil presided at the hiding of the money, and took it under his guardianship; but this, it is well known, he always does with buried treasure, particularly when it has been ill gotten. Be that as it may, Kidd never returned to recover his wealth; being shortly after seized at Boston, sent out to England, and there hanged for a pirate.

About the year 1727, just at the time when earthquakes were prevalent in New England, and shook many tall sinners down upon their knees, there lived near this place a meagre miserly fellow of the name of Tom Walker. He had a wife as miserly as himself; they were so miserly that they even conspired to cheat each other. Whatever the woman could lay hands on she hid away: a hen could not cackle but she was on the alert to secure the new-laid egg. Her husband was continually prying about to detect her secret hoards, and many and fierce were the conflicts that took place about what ought to have been common property. They lived in a forlorn looking house, that stood alone and had an air of starvation. A few straggling savin trees, emblems of sterility, grew near it; no smoke ever curled from its chimney; no traveller stopped at its door. A miserable horse, whose ribs were as articulate as the bars of a gridiron, stalked about a field where a thin carpet of moss, scarcely covering the ragged beds of pudding stone, tantalized and balked his hunger; and sometimes he would lean his head over the fence, look piteously at the passer by, and seem to petition deliverance from this land of famine. The house and its inmates had altogether a bad name. Tom's wife was a tall termagant, fierce of temper, loud of tongue, and strong of arm. Her voice was often heard in wordy warfare with her husband; and his face sometimes showed signs that their conflicts were not confined to words. No one ventured, however, to interfere between them; the lonely wayfarer shrunk within himself at the horrid clamour and clapper clawing; eyed the den of discord askance, and hurried on his way, rejoicing, if a bachelor, in his celibacy.

One day that Tom Walker had been to a distant part of the neighbourhood, he took what he considered a short cut homewards through the swamp. Like most short cuts, it was an ill chosen route. The swamp was thickly grown with great gloomy pines and hemlocks, some of them ninety feet high; which made it dark at noonday, and a retreat for all the owls of the neighbourhood. It was full of pits and quagmires, partly covered with weeds and mosses; where the green surface often betrayed the traveller into a gulf of black smothering mud; there were also dark and stagnant pools, the abodes of the tadpole, the bull-frog, and the water snake, and where trunks of pines and hemlocks lay half drowned, half rotting, looking like alligators, sleeping in the mire.

Tom had long been picking his way cautiously through this treacherous forest; stepping from tuft to tuft of rushes and roots which afforded precarious footholds among deep sloughs; or pacing carefully, like a cat, along the prostrate trunks of trees; startled now and then by the sudden screaming of the bittern, or the quacking of a wild duck, rising on the wing from some solitary pool. At length he arrived at a piece of firm ground, which ran out like a peninsula into the deep bosom of the swamp. It had been one of the strong holds of the Indians during their wars with the first colonists. Here they had thrown up a kind of fort which they had looked upon as almost impregnable, and had used as a place of refuge for their squaws and children. Nothing remained of the Indian fort but a few embankments gradually sinking to the level of the surrounding earth, and already overgrown in part by oaks and other forest trees, the foliage of which formed a contrast to the dark pines and hemlocks of the swamp.

It was late in the dusk of evening that Tom Walker reached the old fort, and he paused there for a while to rest himself. Any one but he would have felt unwilling to linger in this lonely melancholy place, for the common people had a bad opinion of it from the stories handed down from the time of the Indian wars; when it was asserted that the savages held incantations here and made sacrifices to the evil spirit. Tom Walker, however, was not a man to be troubled with any fears of the kind.

He reposed himself for some time on the trunk of a fallen hemlock, listening to the boding cry of the tree toad, and delving with his walking staff into a mound of black mould at his feet. As he turned up the soil unconsciously, his staff struck against something hard. He raked it out of the vegetable mould, and lo! a cloven skull with an Indian tomahawk buried deep in it, lay before him. The rust on the weapon showed the time that had elapsed memento of the fierce struggle that had taken place in this last foothold of the Indian warriors.

"Humph!" said Tom Walker, as he gave the skull a kick to shake the dirt from it.

"Let that skull alone!" said a gruff voice.

Tom lifted up his eyes and beheld a great black man, seated directly opposite him on the stump of a tree. He was exceedingly surprised, having neither seen nor heard any one approach, and he was still more perplexed on observing, as well as the gathering gloom would permit, that the stranger was neither negro nor Indian. It is true, he was dressed in a rude, half Indian garb, and had a red belt or sash swathed round his body, but his face was neither black nor copper colour, but swarthy and dingy and begrimed with soot, as if he had been accustomed to toil among fires and forges. He had a shock of coarse black hair, that stood out from his head in all directions; and bore an axe on his shoulder.

He scowled for a moment at Tom with a pair of great red eyes.

"What are you doing in my grounds?" said the black man, with a hoarse growling voice.

"Your grounds?" said Tom, with a sneer; "no more your grounds than mine: they belong to Deacon Peabody."

"Deacon Peabody be d——d," said the stranger, "as I flatter myself he will be, if he does not look more to his own sins and less to his neighbour's. Look yonder, and see how Deacon Peabody is faring."

Tom looked in the direction that the stranger pointed, and beheld one of the great trees, fair and flourishing without, but rotten at the core, and saw that it had been nearly hewn through, so that the first wind was likely to blow it down. On the bark of the tree was scored the name of Deacon Peabody. He now looked round, and found most of the tall trees marked with the name of some great man of the colony, more or less scored by the axe. The one on which he had been seated, and which had evidently just been hewn down, bore the name of Crowninshield; and he recollected a mighty rich man of that name, who made a vulgar display of wealth, which it was whispered he had acquired by buccaneering.

"He's just ready for burning!" said the black man, with a growl of triumph. "You see I am likely to have a good stock of firewood for winter."

"But what right have you," said Tom, "to cut down Deacon Peabody's timber?"

"The right of prior claim," said the other. "This woodland belonged to me long before one of your white faced race put foot upon the soil."

"And pray, who are you, if I may be so bold?" said Tom.

"Oh, I go by various names. I am the Wild Huntsman in some countries; the Black Miner in others. In this neighbourhood I am known by the name of the Black Woodsman. I am he to whom the red men devoted this spot, and now and then roasted a white man by way of sweet smelling sacrifice. Since the red men have been exterminated by you white savages, I amuse myself by presiding at the persecutions of quakers and anabaptists; I am the great patron and prompter of slave dealers, and the grand master of the Salem witches."

"The upshot of all which is, that, if I mistake not," said Tom, sturdily, "you are he commonly called Old Scratch."

"The same at your service!" replied the black man, with a half civil nod.

Such was the opening of this interview, according to the old story, though it has almost too familiar an air to be credited. One would think that to meet with such a singular personage in this wild lonely place, would have shaken any man's nerves: but Tom was a hard-minded fellow, not easily daunted, and he had lived so long with a termagant wife, that he did not even fear the devil.

It is said that after this commencement, they had a long and earnest conversation together, as Tom returned homewards. The black man told him of great sums of money which had been buried by Kidd the pirate, under the oak trees on the high ridge not far from the morass. All these were under his command and protected by his power, so that none could find them but such as propitiated his favour. These he offered to place within Tom Walker's reach, having conceived an especial kindness for him: but they were to be had only on certain conditions. What these conditions were, may easily be surmised, though Tom never disclosed them publicly. They must have been very hard, for he required time to think of them, and he was not a man to stick at trifles where money was in view. When they had reached the edge of the swamp the stranger paused.

"What proof have I that all you have been telling me is true?" said Tom.

"There is my signature," said the black man, pressing his finger on Tom's forehead. So saying, he turned off among the thickets of the swamp, and seemed, as Tom said, to go down, down, down, into the earth, until nothing but his head and shoulders could be seen, and so on until he totally disappeared.

When Tom reached home he found the black print of a finger burnt, as it were, into his forehead, which nothing could obliterate.

The first news his wife had to tell him was the sudden death of Absalom Crowninshield the rich buccaneer. It was announced in the papers with the usual flourish, that "a great man had fallen in Israel."

Tom recollected the tree which his black friend had just hewn down, and which was ready for burning. "Let the freebooter roast," said Tom, "who cares!" He now felt convinced that all he had heard and seen was no illusion.

He was not prone to let his wife into his confidence; but as this was an uneasy secret, he willingly shared it with her. All her avarice was awakened at the mention of hidden gold, and she urged her husband to comply with the black man's terms and secure what would make them wealthy for life. However Tom might have felt disposed to sell himself to the devil, he was determined not to do so to oblige his wife; so he flatly refused out of the mere spirit of contradiction. Many and bitter were the quarrels they had on the subject, but the more she talked the more resolute was Tom not to be damned to please her. At length she determined to drive the bargain on her own account, and if she succeeded, to keep all the gain to herself.

Being of the same fearless temper as her husband, she set off for the old Indian fort towards the close of a summer's day. She was many hours absent. When she came back she was reserved and sullen in her replies. She spoke something of a black man whom she had met about twilight, hewing at the root of a tall tree. He was sulky, however, and would not come to terms; she was to go again with a propitiatory offering, but what it was she forebore to say.

The next evening she set off again for the swamp, with her apron heavily laden. Tom waited and waited for her, but in vain: midnight came, but she did not make her appearance; morning, noon, night returned, but still she did not come. Tom now grew uneasy for her safety; especially as he found she had carried off in her apron the silver teapot and spoons and every portable article of value. Another night elapsed, another morning came; but no wife. In a word, she was never heard of more.

What was her real fate nobody knows, in consequence of so many pretending to know. It is one of those facts that have become confounded by a variety of historians. Some asserted that she lost her way among the tangled mazes of the swamp and sunk into some pit or slough; others, more uncharitable, hinted that she had eloped with the household booty, and made off to some other province; while others assert that the tempter had decoyed her into a dismal quagmire on top of which her hat was found lying. In confirmation of this, it was said a great black man with an axe on his shoulder was seen late that very evening coming out of the swamp, carrying a bundle tied in a check apron, with an air of surly triumph.

The most current and probable story, however, observes that Tom Walker grew so anxious about the fate of his wife and his property that he sat out at length to seek them both at the Indian fort. During a long summer's afternoon he searched about the gloomy place, but no wife was to be seen. He called her name repeatedly, but she was no where to be heard. The bittern alone responded to his voice, as he flew screaming by; or the bull frog croaked dolefully from a neighbouring pool. At length, it is said, just in the brown hour of twilight, when the owls began to hoot and the bats to flit about, his attention was attracted by the clamour of carrion crows that were hovering about a cypress tree. He looked and beheld a bundle tied in a check apron and hanging in the branches of the tree; with a great vulture perched hard by, as if keeping watch upon it. He leaped with joy, for he recognized his wife's apron, and supposed it to contain the household valuables.

"Let us get hold of the property," said he, consolingly to himself, "and we will endeavour to do without the woman."

As he scrambled up the tree the vulture spread its wide wings, and sailed off screaming into the deep shadows of the forest. Tom seized the check apron, but, woful sight! found nothing but a heart and liver tied up in it.

Such, according to the most authentic old story, was all that was to be found of Tom's wife. She had probably attempted to deal with the black man as she had been accustomed to deal with her husband; but though a female scold is generally considered a match for the devil, yet in this instance she appears to have had the worst of it. She must have died game however; for it is said Tom noticed many prints of cloven feet deeply stamped about the tree, and several handsful of hair, that looked as if they had been plucked from the coarse black shock of the woodsman. Tom knew his wife's prowess by experience. He shrugged his shoulders as he looked at the signs of a fierce clapper clawing. "Egad," said he to himself, "Old Scratch must have had a tough time of it!"

Tom consoled himself for the loss of his property with the loss of his wife; for he was a man of fortitude. He even felt something like gratitude towards the black woodsman, who he considered had done him a kindness. He sought, therefore, to cultivate a farther acquaintance with him, but for some time without success; the old black legs played shy, for whatever people may think, he is not always to be had for calling for; he knows how to play his cards when pretty sure of his game.

At length, it is said, when delay had whetted Tom's eagerness to the quick, and prepared him to agree to any thing rather than not gain the promised treasure, he met the black man one evening in his usual woodman dress, with his axe on his shoulder, sauntering along the edge of the swamp, and humming a tune. He affected to receive Tom's advance with great indifference, made brief replies, and went on humming his tune.

By degrees, however, Tom brought him to business, and they began to haggle about the terms on which the former was to have the pirate's treasure. There was one condition which need not be mentioned, being generally understood in all cases where the devil grants favours; but there were others about which, though of less importance, he was inflexibly obstinate. He insisted that the money found through his means should be employed in his service. He proposed, therefore, that Tom should employ it in the black traffick; that is to say, that he should fit out a slave ship. This, however, Tom resolutely refused; he was bad enough in all conscience; but the devil himself could not tempt him to turn slave dealer.

Finding Tom so squeamish on this point, he did not insist upon it, but proposed instead that he should turn usurer; the devil being extremely anxious for the increase of usurers, looking upon them as his peculiar people.

To this no objections were made, for it was just to Tom's taste.

"You shall open a broker's shop in Boston next month," said the black man.

"I'll do it to-morrow, if you wish," said Tom Walker.

"You shall lend money at two per cent. a month."

"Egad, I'll charge four!" replied Tom Walker.

"You shall extort bonds, foreclose mortgages, drive the merchant to bankruptcy—"

"I'll drive him to the d——l," cried Tom Walker, eagerly.

"You are the usurer for my money!" said the black legs, with delight. "When will you want the rhino?"

"This very night."

"Done!" said the devil.

"Done!" said Tom Walker. —So they shook hands, and struck a bargain.

A few days' time saw Tom Walker seated behind his desk in a counting house in Boston. His reputation for a ready moneyed man, who would lend money out for a good consideration, soon spread abroad. Every body remembers the days of Governor Belcher, when money was particularly scarce. It was a time of paper credit. The country had been deluged with government bills; the famous Land Bank had been established; there had been a rage for speculating; the people had run mad with schemes for new settlements; for building cities in the wilderness; land jobbers went about with maps of grants, and townships, and Eldorados, lying nobody knew where, but which every body was ready to purchase. In a word, the great speculating fever which breaks out every now and then in the country, had raged to an alarming degree, and every body was dreaming of making sudden fortunes from nothing. As usual the fever had subsided; the dream had gone off, and the imaginary fortunes with it; the patients were left in doleful plight, and the whole country resounded with the consequent cry of "hard times."

At this propitious time of public distress did Tom Walker set up as a usurer in Boston. His door was soon thronged by customers. The needy and the adventurous; the gambling speculator; the dreaming land jobber; the thriftless tradesman; the merchant with cracked credit; in short, every one driven to raise money by desperate means and desperate sacrifices, hurried to Tom Walker.

Thus Tom was the universal friend of the needy, and he acted like a "friend in need;" that is to say, he always exacted good pay and good security. In proportion to the distress of the applicant was the hardness of his terms. He accumulated bonds and mortgages; gradually squeezed his customers closer and closer; and sent them at length, dry as a sponge from his door.

In this way he made money hand over hand; became a rich and mighty man, and exalted his cocked hat upon change. He built himself, as usual, a vast house, out of ostentation; but left the greater part of it unfinished and unfurnished out of parsimony. He even set up a carriage in the fullness of his vain glory, though he nearly starved the horses which drew it; and as the ungreased wheels groaned and screeched on the axle trees, you would have thought you heard the souls of the poor debtors he was squeezing.

As Tom waxed old, however, he grew thoughtful. Having secured the good things of this world, he began to feel anxious about those of the next. He thought with regret on the bargain he had made with his black friend, and set his wits to work to cheat him out of the conditions. He became, therefore, all of a sudden, a violent church goer. He prayed loudly and strenuously as if heaven were to be taken by force of lungs. Indeed, one might always tell when he had sinned most during the week, by the clamour of his Sunday devotion. The quiet christians who had been modestly and steadfastly travelling Zionward, were struck with self reproach at seeing themselves so suddenly outstripped in their career by this new-made convert. Tom was as rigid in religious, as in money matters; he was a stern supervisor and censurer of his neighbours, and seemed to think every sin entered up to their account became a credit on his own side of the page. He even talked of the expediency of reviving the persecution of quakers and anabaptists. In a word, Tom's zeal became as notorious as his riches.

Still, in spite of all this strenuous attention to forms, Tom had a lurking dread that the devil, after all, would have his due. That he might not be taken unawares, therefore, it is said he always carried a small bible in his coat pocket. He had also a great folio bible on his counting house desk, and would frequently be found reading it when people called on business; on such occasions he would lay his green spectacles on the book, to mark the place, while he turned round to drive some usurious bargain.

Some say that Tom grew a little crack brained in his old days, and that fancying his end approaching, he had his horse new shod, saddled and bridled, and buried with his feet uppermost; because he supposed that at the last day the world would be turned upside down; in which case he should find his horse standing ready for mounting, and he was determined at the worst to give his old friend a run for it. This, however, is probably a mere old wives fable. If he really did take such a precaution it was totally superfluous; at least so says the authentic old legend which closes his story in the following manner.

On one hot afternoon in the dog days, just as a terrible black thundergust was coming up, Tom sat in his counting house in his white linen cap and India silk morning gown. He was on the point of foreclosing a mortgage, by which he would complete the ruin of an unlucky land speculator for whom he had professed the greatest friendship. The poor land jobber begged him to grant a few months indulgence. Tom had grown testy and irritated and refused another day.

"My family will be ruined and brought upon the parish," said the land jobber. "Charity begins at home," replied Tom, "I must take care of myself in these hard times."

"You have made so much money out of me," said the speculator.

Tom lost his patience and his piety—"The devil take me," said he, "if I have made a farthing!"

Just then there were three loud knocks at the street door. He stepped out to see who was there. A black man was holding a black horse which neighed and stamped with impatience.

"Tom, you're come for!" said the black fellow, gruffly. Tom shrunk back, but too late. He had left his little bible at the bottom of his coat pocket, and his big bible on the desk buried under the mortgage he was about to forclose: never was sinner taken more unawares. The black man whisked him like a child astride the horse and away he galloped in the midst of a thunder storm. The clerks stuck their pens behind their ears and stared after him from the windows. Away went Tom Walker, dashing down the streets; his white cap bobbing up and down; his morning gown fluttering in the wind, and his steed striking fire out of the pavement at every bound. When the clerks turned to look for the black man he had disappeared.

Tom Walker never returned to foreclose the mortgage. A countryman who lived on the borders of the swamp, reported that in the height of the thunder gust he had heard a great clattering of hoofs and a howling along the road, and that when he ran to the window he just caught sight of a figure, such as I have described, on a horse that galloped like mad across the fields, over the hills and down into the black hemlock swamp towards the old Indian fort; and that shortly after a thunderbolt fell in that direction which seemed to set the whole forest in a blaze.

The good people of Boston shook their heads and shrugged their shoulders, but had been so much accustomed to witches and goblins and tricks of the devil in all kinds of shapes from the first settlement of the colony, that they were not so much horror struck as might have been expected. Trustees were appointed to take charge of Tom's effects. There was nothing, however, to administer upon. On searching his coffers all his bonds and mortgages were found reduced to cinders. In place of gold and silver his iron chest was filled with chips and shavings; two skeletons lay in his stable instead of his half starved horses, and the very next day his great house took fire and was burnt to the ground.

Such was the end of Tom Walker and his ill gotten wealth. Let all griping money brokers lay this story to heart. The truth of it is not to be doubted. The very hole under the oak trees, from whence he dug Kidd's money is to be seen to this day; and the neighbouring swamp and old Indian fort is often haunted in stormy nights by a figure on horseback, in a morning gown and white cap, which is doubtless the troubled spirit of the usurer. In fact, the story has resolved itself into a proverb, and is the origin of that popular saying, prevalent throughout New-England, of "The Devil and Tom Walker."

Legend of Don Munio Sancho de Hinojosa

IN THE cloisters of the ancient Benedictine convent of San Domingo, at Silos, in Castile, are the mouldering yet magnificent monuments of the once powerful and chivalrous family of Hinojosa. Among these reclines the marble figure of a knight, in complete armor, with the hands pressed together, as if in prayer. On one side of his tomb is sculptured in relief a band of Christian cavaliers, capturing a cavalcade of male and female Moors; on the other side, the same cavaliers are represented kneeling before an altar. The tomb, like most of the neighboring monuments, is almost in ruins, and the sculpture is nearly unintelligible, excepting to the keen eye of the antiquary. The story connected with the sepulchre, however, is still preserved in the old Spanish chronicles, and is to the following purport:

In old times, several hundred years ago, there was a noble Castilian cavalier, named Don Munio Sancho de Hinojosa, lord of a border castle, which had stood the brunt of many a Moorish foray. He had seventy horsemen as his household troops, all of the ancient Castilian proof; stark warriors, hard riders, and men of iron; with these he scoured the Moorish lands, and made his name terrible throughout the borders. His castle hall was covered with banners, cimeters, and Moslem helms, the trophies of his prowess. Don Munio was, moreover, a keen huntsman, and rejoiced in hounds of all kinds, steeds for the chase, and hawks for the towering sport of falconry. When not engaged in warfare, his delight was to beat up the neighboring forests; and scarcely ever did he ride forth, without hound and horn, a boar-spear in his hand, or a hawk upon his fist, and an attendant train of huntsmen.

His wife, Dona Maria Palacin, was of a gentle and timid nature, little fitted to be the spouse of so hardy and adventurous a knight; and many a tear did the poor lady shed, when he sallied forth upon his daring enterprises, and many a prayer did she offer up for his safety.

As this doughty cavalier was one day hunting, he stationed himself in a thicket, on the borders of a green glade of the forest, and dispersed his followers to rouse the game, and drive it toward his stand. He had not been here long, when a cavalcade of Moors, of both sexes, came prankling over the forest lawn. They were unarmed, and magnificently dressed in robes of tissue and embroidery, rich shawls of India, bracelets and anklets of gold, and jewels that sparkled in the sun.

At the head of this gay cavalcade rode a youthful cavalier, superior to the rest in dignity and loftiness of demeanor, and in splendor of attire; beside him was a damsel, whose veil, blown aside by the breeze, displayed a face of surpassing beauty, and eyes cast down in maiden modesty, yet beaming with tenderness and joy.

Don Munio thanked his stars for sending him such a prize, and exulted at the thought of bearing home to his wife the glittering spoils of these infidels. Putting his hunting horn to his lips, he gave a blast that rung through the forest. His huntsmen came running from all quarters, and the astonished Moors were surrounded and made captives.

The beautiful Moor wrung her hands in despair, and her female attendants uttered the most piercing cries. The young Moorish cavalier alone retained self-possession. He inquired the name of the Christian knight, who commanded this troop of horsemen. When told that it was Don Munio Sancho de

Hinojosa, his countenance lighted up. Approaching that cavalier, and kissing his hand, "Don Munio Sancho," said he, "I have heard of your fame as a true and valiant knight, terrible in arms, but schooled in the noble virtues of chivalry. Such do I trust to find you. In me you behold Abadil, son of a Moorish alcayde. I am on the way to celebrate my nuptials with this lady; chance has thrown us in your power, but I confide in your magnanimity. Take all our treasure and jewels; demand what ransom you think proper for our persons, but suffer us not to be insulted nor dishonored."

When the good knight heard this appeal, and beheld the beauty of the youthful pair, his heart was touched with tenderness and courtesy. "God forbid," said he, "that I should disturb such happy nuptials. My prisoners in troth shall ye be, for fifteen days, and immured within my castle, where I claim, as conqueror, the right of celebrating your espousals."

So saying, he dispatched one of his fleetest horsemen in advance, to notify Dona Maria Palacin of the coming of this bridal party; while he and his huntsmen escorted the cavalcade, not as captors, but as a guard of honor. As they drew near to the castle, the banners were hung out, and the trumpets sounded from the battlements; and on their nearer approach, the drawbridge was lowered, and Dona Maria came forth to meet them, attended by her ladies and knights, her pages and her minstrels. She took the young bride, Allifra, in her arms, kissed her with the tenderness of a sister, and conducted her into the castle. In the mean time, Don Munio sent forth missives in every direction, and had viands and dainties of all kinds collected from the country round; and the wedding of the Moorish lovers was celebrated with all possible state and festivity. For fifteen days, the castle was given up to joy and revelry. There were tiltings and jousts at the ring, and bull-fights, and banquets, and dances to the sound of minstrelsy. When the fifteen days were at an end, he made the bride and bridegroom magnificent presents, and conducted them and their attendants safely beyond the borders. Such, in old times, were the courtesy and generosity of a Spanish cavalier.

Several years after this event, the king of Castile summoned his nobles to assist him in a campaign against the Moors. Don Munio Sancho was among the first to answer to the call, with seventy horsemen, all stanch and well-tried warriors. His wife, Dona Maria hung about his neck. "Alas, my lord!" exclaimed she, "how often wilt thou tempt thy fate, and when will thy thirst for glory be appeased!"

"One battle more," replied Don Munio, "one battle more, for the honor of Castile, and I here make a vow, that when this is over, I will lay by my sword, and repair with my cavaliers in pilgrimage to the sepulchre of our Lord at Jerusalem." The cavaliers all joined with him in the vow, and Dona Maria felt in some degree soothed in spirit; still, she saw with a heavy heart the departure of her husband, and watched his banner with wistful eyes, until it disappeared among the trees of the forest.

The king of Castile led his army to the plains of Salmanara, where they encountered the Moorish host, near to Ucles. The battle was long and bloody; the Christians repeatedly wavered, and were as often rallied by the energy of their commanders. Don Munio was covered with wounds, but refused to leave the field. The Christians at length gave way, and the king was hardly pressed, and in danger of being captured.

Don Munio called upon his cavaliers to follow him to the rescue. "Now is the time," cried he, "to prove your loyalty. Fall to, like brave men! We fight for the true faith, and if we lose our lives here, we gain a better life hereafter."

Rushing with his men between the king and his pursuers, they checked the latter in their career, and gave time for their monarch to escape; but they fell victims to their loyalty. They all fought to the last gasp. Don Munio was singled out by a powerful Moorish knight, but having been wounded in the right arm, he fought to disadvantage, and was slain. The battle being over, the Moor paused to possess himself of the spoils of this redoubtable Christian warrior. When he unlaced the helmet, however, and beheld the countenance of Don Munio, he gave a great cry, and smote his breast. "Woe is me!" cried he, "I have slain my benefactor! The flower of knightly virtue! the most magnanimous of cavaliers!"

While the battle had been raging on the plain of Salmanara, Dona Maria Palacin remained in her castle, a prey to the keenest anxiety. Her eyes were ever fixed on the road that led from the country of the Moors, and often she asked the watchman of the tower, "What seest thou?"

One evening, at the shadowy hour of twilight, the warden sounded his horn. "I see," cried he, "a numerous train winding up the valley. There are mingled Moors and Christians. The banner of my lord is in the advance. Joyful tidings!" exclaimed the old seneschal: "my lord returns in triumph, and brings captives!" Then the castle courts rang with shouts of joy; and the standard was displayed, and the trumpets were sounded, and the draw-bridge was lowered, and Dona Maria went forth with her ladies, and her knights, and her pages, and her minstrels, to welcome her lord from the wars. But as the train drew nigh, she beheld a sumptuous bier, covered with black velvet, and on it lay a warrior, as if taking his repose: he lay in his armor, with his helmet on his head, and his sword in his hand, as one who had never been conquered, and around the bier were the escutcheons of the house of Hinojosa.

A number of Moorish cavaliers attended the bier, with emblems of mourning, and with dejected countenances; and their leader cast himself at the feet of Dona Maria, and hid his face in his hands. She beheld in him the gallant Abadil, whom she had once welcomed with his bride to her castle; but who now came with the body of her lord, whom he had unknowingly slain in battle I.

The sepulchre erected in the cloisters of the convent of San Domingo, was achieved at the expense of the Moor Abadil, as a feeble testimony of his grief for the death of the good knight Don Munio, and his reverence for his memory. The tender and faithful Dona Maria soon followed her lord to the tomb. On one of the stones of a small arch, beside his sepulchre, is the following simple inscription: "Hic jacet Maria Palacin, uxor Munonis Sancij De Finojosa": "Here lies Maria Palacin, wife of Munio Sancho de Hinojosa."

The legend of Don Munio Sancho does not conclude with his death. On the same day on which the battle took place on the plain of Salmanara, a chaplain of the Holy Temple at Jerusalem, while standing at the outer gate, beheld a train of Christian cavaliers advancing, as if in pilgrimage. The chaplain was a native of Spain, and as the pilgrims approached, he knew the foremost to be Don Munio Sancho de Hinojosa, with whom he had been well acquainted in former times. Hastening to the patriarch, he told him of the honorable rank of the pilgrims at the gate. The patriarch, therefore, went forth with a grand procession of priests and monks, and received the pilgrims with all due honor. There were seventy cavaliers, beside their leader, all stark and lofty warriors. They carried their helmets in their hands, and their faces were deadly pale. They greeted no one, nor looked either to the right or to the left, but entered the chapel, and kneeling before the sepulchre of our Saviour, performed their orisons in silence. When they had concluded, they rose as if to depart, and the patriarch and his attendants advanced to speak to them, but they were no more to be seen. Every one marvelled what could be the meaning of this prodigy. The patriarch carefully noted down the day, and sent to Castile to learn tidings of Don Munio Sancho de Hinojosa. He received for reply, that on the very day specified, that worthy knight, with seventy of his followers, had been slain in battle. These, therefore, must have been the blessed spirits of those Christian warriors, come to fulfil their vow of pilgrimage to the Holy Sepulchre at Jerusalem. Such was Castilian faith, in the olden time, which kept its word, even beyond the grave.

If any one should doubt of the miraculous apparition of these phantom knights, let him consult the History of the Kings of Castile and Leon, by the learned and pious Fray Prudencio de Sandoval, bishop of Pamplona, where he will find it recorded in the History of King Don Alonzo VI, on the hundred and second page. It is too precious a legend, to be lightly abandoned to the doubter.

The Tower of Las Infantas

IN AN evening's stroll up a narrow glen, overshadowed by
fig trees, pomegranates, and myrtles, which divides the
lands of the fortress from those of the Generalife, I was
struck with the romantic appearance of a Moorish tower in the
outer wall of the Alhambra, rising high above the tree-tops, and
catching the ruddy rays of the setting sun. A solitary window at
a great height commanded a view of the glen; and as I was re-
garding it, a young female looked out, with her head adorned
with flowers. She was evidently superior to the usual class of
people inhabiting the old towers of the fortress; and this sudden and picturesque glimpse of her reminded me of the descriptions of captive beauties in fairy tales. These fanciful
associations were increased on being informed by my attendant Mateo, that this was the Tower of the Princesses (la Torre
de las Infantas); so called, from having been, according to tra-
dition, the residence of the daughters of the Moorish kings. I
have since visited the tower. It is not generally shown to strangers, though well worthy attention, for the interior is equal,
for beauty of architecture, and delicacy of ornament, to any
part of the palace. The elegance of the central hall, with its
marble fountain, its lofty arches, and richly fretted dome; the
arabesques and stucco-work of the small but well-proportioned
chambers, though injured by time and neglect, all accord with
the story of its being anciently the abode of royal beauty.

The little old fairy queen who lives under the staircase of the
Alhambra, and frequents the evening tertulias of Dame Antonia,

tells some fanciful traditions about three Moorish princesses, who were once shut up in this tower by their father, a tyrant king of Granada, and were only permitted to ride out at night about the hills, when no one was permitted to come in their way under pain of death. They still, according to her account, may be seen occasionally when the moon is in the full, riding in lonely places along the mountain side, on palfreys richly caparisoned and sparkling with jewels, but they vanish on being spoken to.

But before I relate any thing further respecting these princesses, the reader may be anxious to know something about the fair inhabitant of the tower with her head dressed with flowers, who looked out from the lofty window. She proved to be the newly-married spouse of the worthy adjutant of invalids; who, though well stricken in years, had had the courage to take to his bosom a young and buxom Andalusian damsel. May the good old cavalier be happy in his choice, and find the Tower of the Princesses a more secure residence for female beauty than it seems to have proved in the time of the Moslems, if we may believe the following legend!

Legend of the
Three Beautiful Princesses

IN OLD times there reigned a Moorish king in Granada, whose name was Mohamed, to which his subjects added the appellation of El Hayzari, or "The Left-handed." Some say he was so called on account of his being really more expert with his sinister than his dexter hand; others, because he was prone to take every thing by the wrong end; or in other words, to mar wherever he meddled. Certain it is, either through misfortune or mismanagement, he was continually in trouble: thrice was he driven from his throne, and, on one occasion, barely escaped to Africa with his life, in the disguise of a fisherman.[1] Still he was as brave as he was blundering; and though left-handed, wielded his cimeter to such purpose, that he each time re-established himself upon his throne by dint of hard fighting. Instead, however, of learning wisdom from adversity, he hardened his neck, and stiffened his left arm in wilfulness. The evils of a public nature which he thus brought upon himself and his kingdom may be learned by those who will delve into the Arabian annals of Granada; the present legend deals but with his domestic policy.

As this Mohamed was one day riding forth with a train of his courtiers, by the foot of the mountain of Elvira, he met a band of horsemen returning from a foray into the land of the Christians. They were conducting a long string of mules laden

[1] The reader will recognize the sovereign connected with the fortunes of the Abencerrages. His story appears to be a little fictionized in the legend.

with spoil, and many captives of both sexes, among whom the monarch was struck with the appearance of a beautiful damsel, richly attired, who sat weeping on a low palfrey, and heeded not the consoling words of a duenna who rode beside her.

The monarch was struck with her beauty, and, on inquiring of the captain of the troop, found that she was the daughter of the alcayde of a frontier fortress, that had been surprised and sacked in the course of the foray. Mohamed claimed her as his royal share of the booty, and had her conveyed to his harem in the Alhambra. There every thing was devised to soothe her melancholy; and the monarch, more and more enamored, sought to make her his queen. The Spanish maid at first repulsed his addresses—he was an infidel—he was the open foe of her country—what was worse, he was stricken in years!

The monarch, finding his assiduities of no avail, determined to enlist in his favor the duenna, who had been captured with the lady. She was an Andalusian by birth, whose Christian name is forgotten, being mentioned in Moorish legends by no other appellation than that of the discreet Kadiga—and discreet in truth she was, as her whole history makes evident. No sooner had the Moorish king held a little private conversation with her, than she saw at once the cogency of his reasoning, and undertook his cause with her young mistress.

"Go to, now!" cried she; "what is there in all this to weep and wail about? Is it not better to be mistress of this beautiful palace, with all its gardens and fountains, than to be shut up within your father's old frontier tower? As to this Mohamed being an infidel, what is that to the purpose? You marry him, not his religion: and if he is waxing a little old, the sooner will you be a widow, and mistress of yourself; at any rate, you are in his power, and must either be a queen or a slave. When in the hands of a robber, it is better to sell one's merchandise for a fair price, than to have it taken by main force."

The arguments of the discreet Kadiga prevailed. The Spanish lady dried her tears, and became the spouse of Mohamed the Left-handed; she even conformed, in appearance, to the faith of her royal husband; and her discreet duenna immediately became a zealous convert to the Moslem doctrines: it was then the latter received the Arabian name of Kadiga, and was permitted to remain in the confidential employ of her mistress.

In due process of time the Moorish king was made the proud and happy father of three lovely daughters, all born at a birth: he could have wished they had been sons, but consoled himself with the idea that three daughters at a birth were pretty well for a man somewhat stricken in years, and left-handed!

As usual with all Moslem monarchs, he summoned his astrologers on this happy event. They cast the nativities of the three princesses, and shook their heads. "Daughters, O king!" said they, "are always precarious property; but these will most need your watchfulness when they arrive at a marriageable age; at that time gather them under your wings, and trust them to no other guardianship."

Mohamed the Left-handed was acknowledged to be a wise king by his courtiers, and was certainly so considered by himself. The prediction of the astrologers caused him but little disquiet, trusting to his ingenuity to guard his daughters and outwit the Fates.

The three-fold birth was the last matrimonial trophy of the monarch; his queen bore him no more children, and died within a few years, bequeathing her infant daughters to his love, and to the fidelity of the discreet Kadiga.

Many years had yet to elapse before the princesses would arrive at that period of danger—the marriageable age: "It is good, however, to be cautious in time," said the shrewd monarch; so he determined to have them reared in the royal castle of Salobrena. This was a sumptuous palace, incrusted, as it were, in a powerful Moorish fortress on the summit of a hill overlooking the Mediterranean sea. It was a royal retreat, in which the Moslem monarchs shut up such of their relatives, as might endanger their safety; allowing them all kinds of luxuries and amusements, in the midst of which they passed their lives in voluptuous indolence.

Here the princesses remained, immured from the world, but surrounded by enjoyment, and attended by female slaves who anticipated their wishes. They had delightful gardens for their recreation, filled with the rarest fruits and flowers, with aromatic groves and perfumed baths. On three sides the castle looked down upon a rich valley, enamelled with all kinds of culture, and bounded by the lofted Alpuxarra mountains; on the other side it overlooked the broad sunny sea.

In this delicious abode, in a propitious climate, and under a cloudless sky, the three princesses grew up into wondrous beauty; but, though all reared alike, they gave early tokens of diversity of character. Their names were Zayda, Zorayda, and Zorahayda; and such was their order of seniority, for there had been precisely three minutes between their births.

Zayda, the eldest, was of an intrepid spirit, and took the lead of her sisters in every thing, as she had done in entering into the world. She was curious and inquisitive, and fond of getting at the bottom of things.

Zorayda had a great feeling for beauty, which was the reason, no doubt, of her delighting to regard her own image in a mirror or a fountain, and of her fondness for flowers, and jewels, and other tasteful ornaments.

As to Zorahayda, the youngest, she was soft and timid, and extremely sensitive, with a vast deal of disposable tenderness, as was evident from her number of pet-flowers, and pet-birds, and pet-animals, all of which she cherished with the fondest care. Her amusements, too, were of a gentle nature, and mixed up with musing and reverie. She would sit for hours in a balcony, gazing on the sparkling stars of a summer's night, or on the sea when lit up by the moon; and at such times, the song of a fisherman, faintly heard from the beach, or the notes of a Moorish flute from some gliding bark, sufficed to elevate her feelings into ecstasy. The least uproar of the elements, however, filled her with dismay; and a clap of thunder was enough to throw her into a swoon.

Years rolled on smoothly and serenely; the discreet Kadiga, to whom the princesses were confided, was faithful to her trust, and attended them with unremitting care.

The castle of Salobrena, as has been said, was built upon a hill on the seacoast. One of the exterior walls straggled down the profile of the hill, until it reached a jutting rock overhanging the sea, with a narrow sandy beach at its foot, laved by the rippling billows. A small watchtower on this rock had been fitted up as a pavilion, with latticed windows to admit the sea-breeze. Here the princesses used to pass the sultry hours of mid-day.

The curious Zayda was one day seated at a window of the pavilion, as her sisters, reclining on ottomans, were taking the siesta or noontide slumber. Her attention was attracted to a galley which came coasting along, with measured strokes of the oar. As it drew near, she observed that it was filled with armed men. The galley anchored at the foot of the tower: a number of Moorish soldiers landed on the narrow beach, conducting several Christian prisoners. The curious Zayda awakened her sisters, and all three peeped cautiously through the close jalousies of the lattice which screened them from sight. Among the prisoners were three Spanish cavaliers, richly dressed. They were in the flower of youth, and of noble presence; and the lofty manner in which they carried themselves, though loaded with chains and surrounded with enemies, bespoke the grandeur of their souls. The princesses gazed with intense and breathless interest. Cooped up as they had been in this castle among female attendants, seeing nothing of the male sex but black slaves, or the rude fishermen of the sea-coast, it is not to be wondered at that the appearance of three gallant cavaliers, in the pride of youth and manly beauty, should produce some commotion in their bosom.

"Did ever nobler being tread the earth than that cavalier in crimson?" cried Zayda, the eldest of the sisters. "See how proudly he bears himself, as though all around him were his slaves!"

"But notice that one in green!" exclaimed Zorayda. "What grace! what elegance! what spirit!"

The gentle Zorahayda said nothing, but she secretly gave preference to the cavalier in blue.

The princesses remained gazing until the prisoners were out of sight; then heaving long-drawn sighs, they turned round, looked at each other for a moment, and sat down, musing and pensive, on their ottomans.

The discreet Kadiga found them in this situation; they related what they had seen, and even the withered heart of the duenna was warmed. "Poor youths!" exclaimed she, "I'll warrant their captivity makes many a fair and high-born lady's heart ache in their native land! Ah my children, you have little idea of the life these cavaliers lead in their own country. Such prankling at tournaments! such devotion to the ladies! such courting and serenading!"

The curiosity of Zayda was fully aroused; she was insatiable in her inquiries, and drew from the duenna the most animated pictures of the scenes of her youthful days and native land. The beautiful Zorayda bridled up, and slyly regarded herself in a mirror, when the theme turned upon the charms of the Spanish ladies; while Zorahayda suppressed a struggling sigh at the mention of moonlight serenades.

Every day the curious Zayda renewed her inquiries, and every day the sage duenna repeated her stories, which were listened to with profound interest, though with frequent sighs, by her gentle auditors. The discreet old woman awoke at length to the mischief she might be doing. She had been accustomed to think of the princesses only as children; but they had imperceptibly ripened beneath her eye, and now bloomed before her three lovely damsels of the marriageable age. It is time, thought the duenna, to give notice to the king.

Mohamed the Left-handed was seated one morning on a divan in a cool hall of the Alhambra, when a slave arrived from the fortress of Salobrena, with a message from the sage Kadiga, congratulating him on the anniversary of his daughters' birthday. The slave at the same time presented a delicate little basket decorated with flowers, within which, on a couch of vine and fig-leaves, lay a peach, an apricot, and a nectarine, with their bloom and down and dewy sweetness upon them, and all in the early stage of tempting ripeness. The monarch was versed in the Oriental language of fruits and flowers, and rapidly divined the meaning of this emblematical offering.

"So," said he, "the critical period pointed out by the astrologers is arrived: my daughters are at a marriageable age. What is to be done? They are shut up from the eyes of men; they are under the eyes of the discreet Kadiga—all very good—but still they are not under my own eye, as was prescribed by the astrologers: I must gather them under my wing, and trust to no other guardianship."

So saying, he ordered that a tower of the Alhambra should be prepared for their reception, and departed at the head of his guards for the fortress of Salobrena, to conduct them home in person.

About three years had elapsed since Mohamed had beheld his daughters, and he could scarcely credit his eyes at the wonderful change which that small space of time had made in their appearance. During the interval, they had passed that wondrous boundary line in female life which separates the crude, unformed, and thoughtless girl from the blooming, blushing, meditative woman. It is like passing from the flat, bleak, uninteresting plains of La Mancha to the voluptuous valleys and swelling hills of Andalusia.

Zayda was tall and finely formed, with a lofty demeanor and a penetrating eye. She entered with a stately and decided step, and made a profound reverence to Mohamed, treating him more as her sovereign than her father. Zorayda was of the middle height, with an alluring look and swimming gait, and a sparkling beauty, heightened by the assistance of the toilette. She approached her father with a smile, kissed his hand, and saluted him with several stanzas from a popular Arabian poet, with which the monarch was delighted. Zorahayda was shy and timid, smaller than her sisters, and with a beauty of that tender beseeching kind which looks for fondness and protection. She was little fitted to command, like her elder sister, or to dazzle like the second, but was rather formed to creep to the bosom of manly affection, to nestle within it, and be content. She drew near to her father, with a timid and almost faltering step, and would have taken his hand to kiss, but on looking up into his face, and seeing it beaming with a paternal smile, the tenderness of her nature broke forth, and she threw herself upon his neck.

Mohamed the Left-handed surveyed his blooming daughters with mingled pride and perplexity; for while he exulted in their charms, he bethought himself of the prediction of the astrologers. "Three daughters! three daughters!" muttered he repeatedly to himself, "and all of a marriageable age! Here's tempting Hesperian fruit, that requires a dragon watch!"

He prepared for his return to Granada, by sending heralds

before him, commanding every one to keep out of the road by
which he was to pass, and that all doors and windows should
be closed at the approach of the princesses. This done, he set
forth, escorted by a troop of black horsemen of hideous aspect,
and clad in shining armor.

The princesses rode beside the king, closely veiled, on beautiful white palfreys, with velvet caparisons, embroidered with
gold, and sweeping the ground; the bits and stirrups were of
gold, and the silken bridles adorned with pearls and precious
stones. The palfreys were covered with little silver bells, which
made the most musical tinkling as they ambled gently along.
Woe to the unlucky wight, however, who lingered in the way
when he heard the tinkling of these bells!—the guards were
ordered to cut him down without mercy.

The cavalcade was drawing near to Granada, when it over-
took on the banks of the river Xenil, a small body of Moorish
soldiers with a convoy of prisoners. It was too late for the soldiers to get out of the way, so they threw themselves on their
faces on the earth, ordering their captives to do the like. Among
the prisoners were the three identical cavaliers whom the princesses had seen from the pavilion. They either did not understand, or were too haughty to obey the order, and remained
standing and gazing upon the cavalcade as it approached.

The ire of the monarch was kindled at this flagrant defiance
of his orders. Drawing his cimeter, and pressing forward, he
was about to deal a left-handed blow that might have been fatal
to, at least, one of the gazers, when the princesses crowded
round him, and implored mercy for the prisoners; even the timid
Zorahayda forgot her shyness, and became eloquent in their
behalf. Mohamed paused, with uplifted cimeter, when the captain of the guard threw himself at his feet. "Let not your high-
ness," said he, "do a deed that may cause great scandal
throughout the kingdom. These are three brave and noble

Spanish knights, who have been taken in battle, fighting like lions; they are of high birth, and may bring great ransoms."

"Enough!" said the king. "I will spare their lives, but punish their audacity—let them be taken to the Vermilion Towers, and put to hard labor."

Mohamed was making one of his usual left-handed blunders. In the tumult and agitation of this blustering scene, the veils of the three princesses had been thrown back, and the radiance of their beauty revealed; and in prolonging the parley, the king had given that beauty time to have its full effect. In those days people fell in love much more suddenly than at present, as all ancient stories make manifest: it is not a matter of wonder, therefore, that the hearts of the three cavaliers were completely captured; especially as gratitude was added to their admiration; it is a little singular, however, though no less certain, that each of them was enraptured with a several beauty. As to the princesses, they were more than ever struck with the noble demeanor of the captives, and cherished in their breasts all that they had heard of their valor and noble lineage.

The cavalcade resumed its march; the three princesses rode pensively along on their tinkling palfreys, now and then stealing a glance behind in search of the Christian captives, and the latter were conducted to their allotted prison in the Vermilion Towers.

The residence provided for the princesses was one of the most dainty that fancy could devise. It was in a tower somewhat apart from the main palace of the Alhambra, though connected with it by the wall which encircled the whole summit of the hill. On one side it looked into the interior of the fortress, and had, at its foot, a small garden filled with the rarest flowers. On the other side it overlooked a deep embowered ravine separating the grounds of the Alhambra from those of the Generalife. The interior of the tower was divided into small fairy apartments, beautifully ornamented in the light Arabian style, surrounding a lofty hall, the vaulted roof of which rose almost to the summit of the tower. The walls and the ceilings of the hall were adorned with arabesque and fretwork, sparkling with gold and with brilliant pencilling. In the centre of the marble pavement was an alabaster fountain, set round with aromatic shrubs and flowers, and throwing up a jet of water that cooled the whole edifice and had a lulling sound. Round the hall were suspended cages of gold and silver wire, containing singing-birds of the finest plumage or sweetest note.

The princesses had been represented as always cheerful when in the castle of the Salobrena; the king had expected to see them enraptured with the Alhambra. To his surprise, however, they began to pine, and grow melancholy, and dissatisfied with every thing around them. The flowers yielded them no fragrance, the song of the nightingale disturbed their night's rest, and they were out of all patience with the alabaster fountain with its eternal drop-drop and splash-splash, from morning till night, and from night till morning.

The king, who was somewhat of a testy, tyrannical disposition, took this at first in high dudgeon; but he reflected that his daughters had arrived at an age when the female mind expands and its desires augment. "They are no longer children," said he to himself, "they are women grown, and require suitable objects to interest them." He put in requisition, therefore, all the dressmakers, and the jewellers, and the artificers in gold and silver throughout the Zacatin of Granada, and the princesses were overwhelmed with robes of silk, and tissue, and brocade, and cashmere shawls, and necklaces of pearls and diamonds, and rings, and bracelets, and anklets, and all manner of precious things.

All, however, was of no avail; the princesses continued pale and languid in the midst of their finery, and looked like three blighted rose-buds, drooping from one stalk. The king was at his wits' end. He had in general a laudable confidence in his own judgment, and never took advice. "The whims and caprices of three marriageable damsels, however, are sufficient," said he, "to puzzle the shrewdest head." So for once in his life he called in the aid of counsel.

The person to whom he applied was the experienced duenna.

"Kadiga," said the king, "I know you to be one of the most discreet women in the whole world, as well as one of the most trustworthy; for these reasons I have always continued you about the persons of my daughters. Fathers cannot be too wary in whom they repose such confidence; I now wish you to find out the secret malady that is preying upon the princesses, and to devise some means of restoring them to health and cheerfulness."

Kadiga promised implicit obedience. In fact she knew more of the malady of the princesses than they did themselves. Shutting herself up with them, however, she endeavored to insinuate herself into their confidence.

"My dear children, what is the reason you are so dismal and downcast in so beautiful a place, where you have every thing that heart can wish?"

The princesses looked vacantly round the apartment, and sighed.

"What more, then, would you have? Shall I get you the wonderful parrot that talks all languages, and is the delight of Granada?"

"Odious!" exclaimed the princess Zayda. "A horrid, screaming bird, that chatters words without ideas: one must be without brains to tolerate such a pest."

"Shall I send for a monkey from the rock of Gibraltar, to divert you with his antics?"

"A monkey! faugh!" cried Zorayda; "the detestable mimic of man. I hate the nauseous animal."

"What say you to the famous black singer Casem, from the royal harem, in Morocco? They say he has a voice as fine as a woman's."

"I am terrified at the sight of these black slaves," said the delicate Zorahayda; "besides, I have lost all relish for music."

"Ah! my child, you would not say so," replied the old woman, slyly, "had you heard the music I heard last evening, from the three Spanish cavaliers, whom we met on our journey. But, bless me, children! what is the matter that you blush so, and are in such a flutter?"

"Nothing, nothing, good mother; pray proceed."

"Well; as I was passing by the Vermilion Towers last evening, I saw the three cavaliers resting after their day's labor. One was playing on the guitar, so gracefully, and the others sang by turns; and they did it in such style, that the very guards seemed like statues, or men enchanted. Allah forgive me! I could not help being moved at hearing the songs of my native country. And then to see three such noble and handsome youths in chains and slavery!"

Here the kind-hearted old woman could not restrain her tears.

"Perhaps, mother, you could manage to procure us a sight of these cavaliers," said Zayda.

"I think," said Zorayda, "a little music would be quite reviving."

The timid Zorahayda said nothing, but threw her arms round the neck of Kadiga.

"Mercy on me!" exclaimed the discreet old woman; "what are you talking of, my children? Your father would be the death of us all if he heard of such a thing. To be sure, these cavaliers are evidently well-bred, and high-minded youths; but what of that? they are the enemies of our faith, and you must not even think of them but with abhorrence."

There is an admirable intrepidity in the female will, particularly when about the marriageable age, which is not to be deterred by dangers and prohibitions. The princesses hung round their old duenna, and coaxed, and entreated, and declared that a refusal would break their hearts.

What could she do? She was certainly the most discreet old woman in the whole world, and one of the most faithful servants to the king; but was she to see three beautiful princesses break their hearts for the mere tinkling of a guitar? Besides, though she had been so long among the Moors, and changed her faith in imitation of her mistress, like a trusty follower, yet she was a Spaniard born, and had the lingerings of Christianity in her heart. So she set about to contrive how the wish of the princesses might be gratified.

The Christian captives, confined in the Vermilion Towers, were under the charge of a big-whiskered, broad-shouldered renegado, called Hussein Baba, who was reputed to have a most itching palm. She went to him privately, and slipping a broad piece of gold into his hand, "Hussein Baba," said she; "My mistresses, the three princesses, who are shut up in the tower, and in sad want of amusement, have heard of the musical talents of the three Spanish cavaliers, and are desirous of hearing a specimen of their skill. I am sure you are too kind-hearted to refuse them so innocent a gratification."

"What! and to have my head set grinning over the gate of my own tower! for that would be the reward, if the king should discover it."

"No danger of any thing of the kind; the affair may be managed so that the whim of the princesses may be gratified, and their father be never the wiser. You know the deep ravine outside of the walls which passes immediately below the tower. Put the three Christians to work there, and at the intervals of their labor, let them play and sing, as if for their own recreation. In this way the princesses will be able to hear them from the windows of the tower, and you may be sure of their paying well for your compliance."

As the good old woman concluded her harangue, she kindly pressed the rough hand of the renegado, and left within it another piece of gold.

Her eloquence was irresistible. The very next day the three cavaliers were put to work in the ravine. During the noontide heat, when their fellow-laborers were sleeping in the shade, and the guard nodding drowsily at his post, they seated themselves among the herbage at the foot of the tower, and sang a Spanish roundelay to the accompaniment of the guitar.

The glen was deep, the tower was high, but their voices rose distinctly in the stillness of the summer noon. The princesses listened from their balcony, they had been taught the Spanish language by their duenna, and were moved by the tenderness of the song. The discreet Kadiga, on the contrary, was terribly shocked. "Allah preserve us!" cried she, "they are singing a love-ditty, addressed to yourselves. Did ever mortal hear of such audacity? I will run to the slave-master, and have them soundly bastinadoed."

"What! bastinado such gallant cavaliers, and for singing so charmingly!" The three beautiful princesses were filled with horror at the idea. With all her virtuous indignation, the good old woman was of a placable nature, and easily appeased. Besides, the music seemed to have a beneficial effect upon her young mistresses. A rosy bloom had already come to their cheeks, and their eyes began to sparkle. She made no further objection, therefore, to the amorous ditty of the cavaliers.

When it was finished, the princesses remained silent for a time; at length Zorayda took up a lute, and with a sweet, though faint and trembling voice, warbled a little Arabian air, the burden of which was, "The rose is concealed among her leaves, but she listens with delight to the song of the nightingale."

From this time forward the cavaliers worked almost daily in the ravine. The considerate Hussein Baba became more and more indulgent, and daily more prone to sleep at his post. For some time a vague intercourse was kept up by popular songs and romances, which, in some measure, responded to each other, and breathed the feelings of the parties. By degrees the princesses showed themselves at the balcony, when they could do so without being perceived by the guards. They conversed with the cavaliers also, by means of flowers, with the symbolical language of which they were mutually acquainted. The difficulties of their intercourse added to its charms, and strengthened the passion they had so singularly conceived; for love delights to struggle with difficulties, and thrives the most hardily on the scantiest soil.

The change effected in the looks and spirits of the princesses by this secret intercourse, surprised and gratified the left-handed king; but no one was more elated than the discreet Kadiga, who considered it all owing to her able management.

At length there was an interruption in this telegraphic correspondence; for several days the cavaliers ceased to make their appearance in the glen. The princesses looked out from the tower in vain. In vain they stretched their swan-like necks from the balcony; in vain they sang like captive nightingales in their cage: nothing was to be seen of their Christian lovers; not a note responded from the groves. The discreet Kadiga sallied forth in quest of intelligence, and soon returned with a face full of trouble. "Ah, my children!" cried she, "I saw what all this would come to, but you would have your way; you may now hang up your lutes on the willows. The Spanish cavaliers are ransomed by their families; they are down in Granada, and preparing to return to their native country."

The three beautiful princesses were in despair at the tidings. Zayda was indignant at the slight put upon them, in thus being deserted without a parting word. Zorayda wrung her hands and cried, and looked in the glass, and wiped away her tears, and cried afresh. The gentle Zorahayda leaned over the balcony and wept in silence, and her tears fell drop by drop among the flowers of the bank where the faithless cavaliers had so often been seated.

The discreet Kadiga did all in her power to soothe their sorrow. "Take comfort, my children," said she, "this is nothing when you are used to it. This is the way of the world. Ah! when you are as old as I am, you will know how to value these men. I'll warrant these cavaliers have their loves among the Spanish beauties of Cordova and Seville, and will soon be serenading under their balconies, and thinking no more of the Moorish beauties in the Alhambra. Take comfort, therefore, my children, and drive them from your hearts."

The comforting words of the discreet Kadiga only redoubled the distress of the three princesses, and for two days they continued inconsolable. On the morning of the third, the good old woman entered their apartment, all ruffling with indignation.

"Who would have believed such insolence in mortal man!" exclaimed she, as soon as she could find words to express herself; "but I am rightly served for having connived at this deception of your worthy father. Never talk more to me of your Spanish cavaliers."

"Why, what has happened, good Kadiga?" exclaimed the princesses in breathless anxiety.

"What has happened?—treason has happened! or what is almost as bad, treason has been proposed; and to me, the most faithful of subjects, the trustiest of duennas! Yes, my children, the Spanish cavaliers have dared to tamper with me, that I should persuade you to fly with them to Cordova, and become their wives!"

Here the excellent old woman covered her face with her hands, and gave way to a violent burst of grief and indignation. The three beautiful princesses turned pale and red, pale and red, and trembled, and looked down, and cast shy looks at each other, but said nothing. Meantime, the old woman sat rocking backward and forward in violent agitation, and now and then breaking out into exclamations, "That ever I should live to be so insulted!—I, the most faithful of servants!"

At length, the eldest princess, who had most spirit and always took the lead, approached her, and laying her hand upon her shoulder, "Well, mother," said she, "supposing we were willing to fly with these Christian cavaliers—is such a thing possible?"

The good old woman paused suddenly in her grief, and looking up, "Possible," echoed she; "to be sure, it is possible. Have not the cavaliers already bribed Hussein Baba, the renegado captain of the guard, and arranged the whole plan? But, then, to think of deceiving your father! your father, who has placed such confidence in me!" Here the worthy woman gave way to a fresh burst of grief, and began to rock backward and forward, and to wring her hands.

"But our father has never placed any confidence in us," said the eldest princess, "but has trusted to bolts and bars, and treated us as captives."

"Why, that is true enough," replied the old woman, again pausing in her grief; "he has indeed treated you most unreasonably, keeping you shut up here, to waste your bloom in a moping old tower, like roses left to wither in a flower-jar. But, then, to fly from your native land!"

"And is not the land we fly to, the native land of our mother, where we shall live in freedom? And shall we not each have a youthful husband in exchange for a severe old father?"

"Why, that again is all very true; and your father, I must confess, is rather tyrannical: but what then," relapsing into her grief, "would you leave me behind to bear the brunt of his vengeance?"

"By no means, my good Kadiga; cannot you fly with us?"

"Very true, my child; and, to tell the truth, when I talked the matter over with Hussein Baba, he promised to take care of me, if I would accompany you in your flight: but then, bethink you, my children, are you willing to renounce the faith of your father?"

"The Christian faith was the original faith of our mother," said the eldest princess; "I am ready to embrace it, and so, I am sure, are my sisters."

"Right again," exclaimed the old woman, brightening up; "it was the original faith of your mother, and bitterly did she lament, on her death-bed, that she had renounced it. I promised her then to take care of your souls, and I rejoice to see that they are now in a fair way to be saved. Yes, my children, I, too, was born a Christian, and have remained a Christian in my heart, and am resolved to return to the faith. I have talked on the subject with Hussein Baba, who is a Spaniard by birth, and comes from a place not far from my native town. He is equally anxious to see his own country, and to be reconciled to the church; and the cavaliers have promised, that, if we are disposed to become man and wife, on returning to our native land, they will provide for us handsomely."

In a word, it appeared that this extremely discreet and provident old woman had consulted with the cavaliers and the renegado, and had concerted the whole plan of escape. The eldest princess immediately assented to it; and her example, as usual, determined the conduct of her sisters. It is true, the youngest hesitated, for she was gentle and timid of soul, and there was a struggle in her bosom between filial feeling and youthful passion: the latter, however, as usual, gained the victory, and with silent tears, and stifled sighs, she prepared herself for flight.

The rugged hill on which the Alhambra is built was, in old times, perforated with subterranean passages, cut through the rock, and leading from the fortress to various parts of the city, and to distant sally-ports on the banks of the Darro and the Xenil. They had been constructed at different times by the Moorish kings, as means of escape from sudden insurrections, or of secretly issuing forth on private enterprises. Many of them are now entirely lost, while others remain, partly choked with rubbish, and partly walled up; monuments of the jealous precautions and warlike stratagems of the Moorish government. By one of these passages, Hussein Baba had undertaken to conduct the princesses to a sally-port beyond the walls of the city, where the cavaliers were to be ready with fleet steeds, to bear the whole party over the borders.

The appointed night arrived: the tower of the princesses had been locked up as usual, and the Alhambra was buried in deep sleep. Towards midnight, the discreet Kadiga listened from the balcony of a window that looked into the garden. Hussein Baba, the renegado, was already below, and gave the appointed signal. The duenna fastened the end of a ladder of ropes to the balcony, lowered it into the garden and descended. The two eldest princesses followed her with beating hearts; but when it came to the turn of the youngest princess, Zorahayda, she hesitated, and trembled. Several times she ventured a delicate little foot upon the ladder, and as often drew it back, while her poor little heart fluttered more and more the longer she delayed. She cast a wistful look back into the silken chamber; she had lived in it, to be sure, like a bird in a cage; but within it she was secure; who could tell what dangers might beset her, should she flutter forth into the wide world! Now she bethought her of the gallant Christian lover, and her little foot was instantly upon the ladder; and anon she thought of her father, and shrank back. But fruitless is the attempt to describe the conflict in the bosom of one so young and tender and loving, but so timid, and so ignorant of the world.

In vain her sisters implored, the duenna scolded, and the renegado blasphemed beneath the balcony; the gentle little Moorish maid stood doubting and wavering on the verge of elopement, tempted by the sweetness of the sin, but terrified at its perils.

Every moment increased the danger of discovery. A distant

tramp was heard. "The patrols are walking their rounds," cried the renegado; "if we linger, we perish. Princess, descend instantly, or we leave you."

Zorahayda was for a moment in fearful agitation; then loosening the ladder of ropes, with desperate resolution, she flung it from the balcony.

"It is decided!" cried she; "flight is now out of my power! Allah guide and bless ye, my dear sisters!"

The two eldest princesses were shocked at the thoughts of leaving her behind, and would fain have lingered, but the patrol was advancing; the renegado was furious, and they were hurried away to the subterraneous passage. They groped their way through a fearful labyrinth, cut through the heart of the mountain, and succeeded in reaching, undiscovered, an iron gate that opened outside of the walls. The Spanish cavaliers were waiting to receive them, disguised as Moorish soldiers of the guard, commanded by the renegado.

The lover of Zorahayda was frantic, when he learned that she had refused to leave the tower; but there was no time to waste in lamentations. The two princesses were placed behind their lovers, the discreet Kadiga mounted behind the renegado, and they all set off at a round pace in the direction of the Pass of Lope, which leads through the mountains towards Cordova.

They had not proceeded far when they heard the noise of drums and trumpets from the battlements of the Alhambra.

"Our flight is discovered!" said the renegado.

"We have fleet steeds, the night is dark, and we may distance all pursuit," replied the cavaliers.

They put spurs to their horses, and scoured across the Vega. They attained the foot of the mountain of Elvira, which stretches like a promontory into the plain. The renegado paused and listened. "As yet," said he, "there is no one on our traces, we shall make good our escape to the mountains." While he spoke, a light blaze sprang up on the top of the watchtower of the Alhambra.

"Confusion!" cried the renegado, "that bale fire will put all the guards of the passes on the alert. Away! away! Spur like mad—there is no time to be lost."

Away they dashed—the clattering of their horses' hoofs echoed from rock to rock, as they swept along the road that skirts the rocky mountain of Elvira. As they galloped on, the bale fire of the Alhambra was answered in every direction; light after light blazed on the atalayas, or watchtowers of the mountains.

"Forward! forward!" cried the renegado, with many an oath, "to the bridge—to the bridge, before the alarm has reached there!"

They doubled the promontory of the mountains, and arrived in sight of the famous Bridge of Pinos, that crosses a rushing stream often dyed with Christian and Moslem blood. To their confusion, the tower on the bridge blazed with lights and glittered with armed men. The renegado pulled up his steed, rose in his stirrups and looked about him for a moment; then beckoning to the cavaliers, he struck off from the road, skirted the river for some distance, and dashed into its waters. The cavaliers called upon the princesses to cling to them, and did the same. They were borne for some distance down the rapid current, the surges roared round them, but the beautiful princesses clung to their Christian knights, and never uttered a complaint. The cavaliers attained the opposite bank in safety, and were conducted by the renegado, by rude and unfrequented paths, and wild barrancos, through the heart of the mountains, so as to avoid all the regular passes. In a word, they succeeded in reaching the ancient city of Cordova; where their restoration to their country and friends was celebrated with great rejoicings, for they were of the noblest families. The beautiful princesses were forthwith received into the bosom of the Church, and, after being in all due form made regular Christians, were rendered happy wives.

In our hurry to make good the escape of the princesses across the river, and up the mountains, we forgot to mention the fate of the discreet Kadiga. She had clung like a cat to Hussein Baba in the scamper across the Vega, screaming at every bound, and drawing many an oath from the whiskered renegado; but when he prepared to plunge his steed into the river, her terror knew no bounds. "Grasp me not so tightly," cried Hussein Baba; "hold on by my belt and fear nothing." She held firmly with both hands by the leathern belt that girded the broad-backed renegado; but when he halted with the cavaliers to take breath on the mountain summit, the duenna was no longer to be seen.

"What has become of Kadiga?" cried the princesses in alarm.

"Allah alone knows!" replied the renegado; "my belt came loose when in the midst of the river, and Kadiga was swept with it down the stream. The will of Allah be done! but it was an embroidered belt, and of great price."

There was no time to waste in idle regrets; yet bitterly did the princesses bewail the loss of their discreet counsellor. That excellent old woman, however, did not lose more than half of her nine lives in the water: a fisherman, who was drawing his nets some distance down the stream, brought her to land, and was not a little astonished at his miraculous draught. What further became of the discreet Kadiga, the legend does not mention; certain it is that she evinced her discretion in never venturing within the reach of Mohamed the Left-handed.

Almost as little is known of the conduct of that sagacious monarch when he discovered the escape of his daughters, and the deceit practised upon him by the most faithful of servants. It was the only instance in which he had called in the aid of counsel, and he was never afterwards known to be guilty of a similar weakness. He took good care, however, to guard his remaining daughter, who had no disposition to elope: it is thought, indeed, that she secretly repented having remained behind: now and then she was seen leaning on the battlements of the tower, and looking mournfully towards the mountains in the direction of Cordova, and sometimes the notes of her lute were heard accompanying plaintive ditties, in which she was said to lament the loss of her sisters and her lover, and to bewail her solitary life. She died young, and, according to popular rumor, was buried in a vault beneath the tower, and her untimely fate has given rise to more than one traditionary fable.

The following legend, which seems in some measure to spring out of the foregoing story, is too closely connected with high historic names to be entirely doubted. The Count's daughter, and some of her young companions, to whom it was read in one of the evening tertulias, thought certain parts of it had much appearance of reality; and Dolores, who was much more versed than they in the improbable truths of the Alhambra, believed every word of it.

The Adventure of the Mason

THERE WAS once upon a time a poor mason, or bricklayer, in Granada, who kept all the saints' days and holidays, and Saint Monday into the bargain, and yet, with all his devotion, he grew poorer and poorer, and could scarcely earn bread for his numerous family. One night he was roused from his first sleep by a knocking at his door. He opened it, and beheld before him a tall, meagre, cadaverous-looking priest.

"Hark ye, honest friend!" said the stranger; "I have observed that you are a good Christian, and one to be trusted; will you undertake a job this very night?"

"With all my heart, Senor Padre, on condition that I am paid accordingly."

"That you shall be; but you must suffer yourself to be blind-folded."

To this the mason made no objection; so, being hoodwinked, he was led by the priest through various rough lanes and winding passages, until they stopped before the portal of a house. The priest then applied a key, turned a creaking lock, and opened what sounded like a ponderous door. They entered, the door was closed and bolted, and the mason was conducted through an echoing corridor, and a spacious hall, to an interior part of the building. Here the bandage was removed from his eyes, and he found himself in a patio, or court, dimly lighted by a single lamp. In the centre was the dry basin of an old Moorish fountain, under which the priest requested him to form a small vault, bricks and mortar being at hand for the purpose. He accordingly worked all night, but without finishing the job. Just before daybreak the priest put a piece of gold into his hand, and having again blindfolded him, conducted him back to his dwelling.

"Are you willing," said he, "to return and complete your work?"

"Gladly, Senor Padre, provided I am so well paid."

"Well, then, to-morrow at midnight I will call again."

He did so, and the vault was completed.

"Now," said the priest, "you must help me to bring forth the bodies that are to be buried in this vault."

The poor mason's hair rose on his head at these words: he followed the priest, with trembling steps, into a retired chamber of the mansion, expecting to behold some ghastly spectacle of death, but was relieved on perceiving three or four portly jars standing in one corner. They were evidently full of money, and it was with great labor that he and the priest carried them forth and consigned them to their tomb. The vault was then closed, the pavement replaced, and all traces of the work were obliterated. The mason was again hoodwinked and led forth by a route different from that by which he had come.

After they had wandered for a long time through a perplexed maze of lanes and alleys, they halted. The priest then put two pieces of gold into his hand. "Wait here," said he, "until you hear the cathedral bell toll for matins. If you presume to uncover your eyes before that time, evil will befall you." So saying, he departed.

The mason waited faithfully, amusing himself by weighing the gold pieces in his hand, and clinking them against each other. The moment the cathedral bell rang its matin peal, he uncovered his eyes, and found himself on the banks of the Xenil; whence he made the best of his way home, and revelled with his family for a whole fortnight on the profits of his two nights' work; after which, he was as poor as ever.

He continued to work a little, and pray a good deal, and keep saints' days and holidays, from year to year, while his family grew up as gaunt and ragged as a crew of gipsies. As he was seated one evening at the door of his hovel, he was accosted by a rich old curmudgeon, who was noted for owning many houses, and being a griping landlord. The man of money eyed him for a moment from beneath a pair of anxious shagged eyebrows.

"I am told, friend, that you are very poor."

"There is no denying the fact, senor—it speaks for itself"

"I presume then, that you will be glad of a job, and will work cheap."

"As cheap, my master, as any mason in Granada."

"That's what I want. I have an old house fallen into decay, which costs me more money than it is worth to keep it in repair, for nobody will live in it; so I must contrive to patch it up and keep it together at as small expense as possible."

The mason was accordingly conducted to a large deserted house that seemed going to ruin. Passing through several empty halls and chambers, he entered an inner court, where his eye was caught by an old Moorish fountain. He paused for a moment, for a dreaming recollection of the place came over him.

"Pray," said he, "who occupied this house formerly?"

"A pest upon him!" cried the landlord, "it was an old miserly priest, who cared for nobody but himself He was said to be immensely rich, and, having no relations, it was thought he would leave all his treasures to the church. He died suddenly, and the priests and friars thronged to take possession of his wealth; but nothing could they find but a few ducats in a leathern purse. The worst luck has fallen on me, for, since his death, the old fellow continues to occupy my house without paying rent, and there is no taking the law of a dead man. The people pretend to hear the clinking of gold all night in the chamber where the old priest slept, as if he were counting over his money, and sometimes a groaning and moaning about the court. Whether true or false, these stories have brought a bad name on my house, and not a tenant will remain in it."

"Enough," said the mason sturdily, "let me live in your house rent-free until some better tenant present, and I will engage to put it in repair, and to quiet the troubled spirit that disturbs it. I am a good Christian and a poor man, and am not to be daunted by the Devil himself, even though he should come in the shape of a big bag of money!"

The offer of the honest mason was gladly accepted; he moved with his family into the house, and fulfilled all his engagements. By little and little he restored it to its former state; the clinking of gold was no more heard at night in the chamber of the defunct priest, but began to be heard by day in the pocket of the living mason. In a word, he increased rapidly in wealth, to the admiration of all his neighbors, and became one of the richest men in Granada: he gave large sums to the church, by way, no doubt, of satisfying his conscience, and never revealed the secret of the vault until on his deathbed to his son and heir.

The Governor and the Notary

IN FORMER times there ruled, as governor of the Alhambra, a doughty old cavalier, who, from having lost one arm in the wars, was commonly known by the name of el Gobernador Manco, or "the one-armed governor." He in fact prided himself upon being an old soldier, wore his mustaches curled up to his eyes, a pair of campaigning boots, and a Toledo as long as a spit, with his pocket handkerchief in the basket-hilt.

He was, moreover, exceedingly proud and punctilious, and tenacious of all his privileges and dignities. Under his sway the immunities of the Alhambra, as a royal residence and domain, were rigidly exacted. No one was permitted to enter the fortress with firearms, or even with a sword or staff, unless he were of a certain rank; and every horseman was obliged to dismount at the gate, and lead his horse by the bridle. Now as the hill of the Alhambra rises from the very midst of the city of Granada, being, as it were, an excrescence of the capital, it must at all times be somewhat irksome to the captain-general, who commands the province, to have thus an imperium in imperio, a petty independent post in the very centre of his domains. It was rendered the more galling, in the present instance, from the irritable jealousy of the old governor, that took fire on the least question of authority and jurisdiction; and from the loose vagrant character of the people who had gradually nestled themselves within the fortress, as in a sanctuary, and thence carried on a system of roguery and depredation at the expense of the honest inhabitants of the city.

Thus there was a perpetual feud and heart-burning between the captain-general and the governor, the more virulent on the part of the latter, inasmuch as the smallest of two neighboring potentates is always the most captious about his dignity. The stately palace of the captain-general stood in the Plaza Nueva, immediately at the foot of the hill of the Alhambra, and here was always a bustle and parade of guards, and domestics, and city functionaries. A beetling bastion of the fortress overlooked the palace and public square in front of it; and on this bastion the old governor would occasionally strut backwards and forwards, with his Toledo girded by his side, keeping a wary eye down upon his rival, like a hawk reconnoitering his quarry from his nest in a dry tree.

Whenever he descended into the city it was in grand parade, on horseback, surrounded by his guards, or in his state coach, an ancient and unwieldy Spanish edifice of carved timber and gilt leather, drawn by eight mules, with running footmen, outriders, and lackeys; on which occasions he flattered himself he impressed every beholder with awe and admiration as vicegerent of the king; though the wits of Granada, particularly those who loitered about the palace of the captain-general, were apt to sneer at his petty parade, and in allusion to the vagrant character of his subjects, to greet him with the appellation of "the king of the beggars." One of the most fruitful sources of dispute between these two doughty rivals was the right claimed by the governor to have all things passed free of duty through the city, that were intended for the use of himself or his garrison. By degrees this privilege had given rise to extensive smuggling. A nest of contrabandistas took up their abode in the hovels of the fortress, and the numerous caves in its vicinity, and drove a thriving business under the connivance of the soldiers of the garrison.

The vigilance of the captain-general was aroused. He consulted his legal adviser and factotum, a shrewd meddlesome escribano, or notary, who rejoiced in an opportunity of perplexing the old potentate of the Alhambra, and involving him in a maze of legal subtilties. He advised the captain-general to insist upon the right of examining every convoy passing through the gates of his city, and penned a long letter for him in vindication of the right. Governor Manco was a straightforward cut-and-thrust old soldier, who hated an escribano worse than the devil and this one in particular worse than all other escribanos.

"What!" said he, curling up his mustaches fiercely, "does the captain-general set his man of the pen to practise confusions upon me? I'll let him see an old soldier is not to be baffled by schoolcraft."

He seized his pen and scrawled a short letter in a crabbed hand, in which, without deigning to enter into argument, he insisted on the right of transit free of search, and denounced vengeance on any custom-house officer who should lay his unhallowed hand on any convoy protected by the flag of the Alhambra. While this question was agitated between the two pragmatical potentates, it so happened that a mule laden with supplies for the fortress arrived one day at the gate of Xenil, by which it was to traverse a suburb of the city on its way to the Alhambra. The convoy was headed by a testy old corporal, who had long served under the governor, and was a man after his own heart; as rusty and stanch as an old Toledo blade.

As they approached the gate of the city, the corporal placed the banner of the Alhambra on the pack-saddle of the mule, and drawing himself up to a perfect perpendicular, advanced with his head dressed to the front, but with the wary side-glance of a cur passing through hostile ground, and ready for a snap and a snarl.

"Who goes there?" said the sentinel at the gate.

"Soldier of the Alhambra!" said the corporal, without turning his head.

"What have you in charge?"

"Provisions for the garrison."

"Proceed."

The corporal marched straight forward, followed by the convoy, but had not advanced many paces before a posse of custom-house officers rushed out of a small toll-house.

"Hallo there!" cried the leader. "Muleteer, halt, and open those packages."

The corporal wheeled round, and drew himself up in battle array. "Respect the flag of the Alhambra," said he; "these things are for the governor."

"A figo for the governor, and a figo for his flag. Muleteer, halt, I say."

"Stop the convoy at your peril!" cried the corporal, cocking his musket.

The muleteer gave his beast a hearty thwack; the custom-house officer sprang forward and seized the halter; whereupon the corporal levelled his piece, and shot him dead.

The street was immediately in an uproar.

The old corporal was seized, and after undergoing sundry kicks, and cuffs, and cudgellings, which are generally given impromptu by the mob in Spain, as a foretaste of the after penalties of the law, he was loaded with irons, and conducted to the city prison; while his comrades were permitted to proceed with the convoy, after it had been well rummaged, to the Alhambra.

The old governor was in a towering passion when he heard of this insult to his flag and capture of his corporal. For a time he stormed about the Moorish halls, and vapored about the bastions, and looked down fire and sword upon the palace of the captain-general. Having vented the first ebullition of his wrath, he dispatched a message demanding the surrender of the corporal, as to him alone belonged the right of sitting in judgment on the offences of those under his command. The captain-general, aided by the pen of the delighted escribano, replied at great length, arguing that as the offence had been committed within the walls of his city, and against one of his civil officers, it was clearly within his proper jurisdiction. The governor rejoined by a repetition of his demand; the captain-general gave a sur-rejoinder of still greater length and legal acumen; the governor became hotter and more peremptory in his demands, and the captain-general cooler and more copious in his replies; until the old lion-hearted soldier absolutely roared with fury at being thus entangled in the meshes of legal controversy.

While the subtle escribano was thus amusing himself at the expense of the governor, he was conducting the trial of the corporal, who, mewed up in a narrow dungeon of the prison, had merely a small grated window at which to show his iron-bound visage and receive the consolations of his friends.

A mountain of written testimony was diligently heaped up, according to Spanish form, by the indefatigable escribano; the corporal was completely overwhelmed by it. He was convicted of murder, and sentenced to be hanged.

It was in vain the governor sent down remonstrance and menace from the Alhambra. The fatal day was at hand, and the corporal was put in capilla, that is to say, in the chapel of the prison, as is always done with culprits the day before execution, that they may meditate on their approaching end and repent them of their sins.

Seeing things drawing to extremity, the old governor determined to attend to the affair in person. For this purpose he ordered out his carriage of state, and, surrounded by his guards, rumbled down the avenue of the Alhambra into the city. Driving to the house of the escribano, he summoned him to the portal.

The eye of the old governor gleamed like a coal at beholding the smirking man of the law advancing with an air of exultation.

"What is this I hear," cried he, "that you are about to put to death one of my soldiers?"

"All according to law—all in strict form of justice," said the self-sufficient escribano, chuckling and rubbing his hands. "I can show your excellency the written testimony in the case."

"Fetch it hither," said the governor. The escribano bustled into his office, delighted with having another opportunity of displaying his ingenuity at the expense of the hard-headed veteran.

He returned with a satchel full of papers, and began to read a long deposition with professional volubility. By this time a crowd had collected, listening with outstretched necks and gaping mouths.

"Prithee, man, get into the carriage, out of this pestilent throng, that I may the better hear thee," said the governor.

The escribano entered the carriage, when, in a twinkling, the door was closed, the coachman smacked his whip—mules, carriage, guards and all dashed off at a thundering rate, leaving the crowd in gaping wonderment; nor did the governor pause until he had lodged his prey in one of the strongest dungeons of the Alhambra.

He then sent down a flag of truce in military style, proposing a cartel or exchange of prisoners—the corporal for the notary. The pride of the captain-general was piqued; he returned a contemptuous refusal, and forthwith caused a gallows, tall and strong, to be erected in the centre of the Plaza Nueva for the execution of the corporal.

"Oho! is that the game?" said Governor Manco. He gave orders, and immediately a gibbet was reared on the verge of the great beetling bastion that overlooked the Plaza. "Now," said he in a message to the captain-general, "hang my soldier when you please; but at the same time that he is swung off in the square, look up to see your escribano dangling against the sky."

The captain-general was inflexible; troops were paraded in the square; the drums beat, the bell tolled. An immense multitude of amateurs gathered together to behold the execution. On the other hand, the governor paraded his garrison on the bastion, and tolled the funeral dirge of the notary from the Torre de la Campana, or Tower of the Bell.

The notary's wife pressed through the crowd with a whole progeny of little embryo escribanos at her heels, and throwing herself at the feet of the captain-general, implored him not to sacrifice the life of her husband, and the welfare of herself and her numerous little ones, to a point of pride; "for you know the old governor too well," said she, "to doubt that he will put his threat in execution, if you hang the soldier."

The captain-general was overpowered by her tears and lamentations, and the clamors of her callow brood. The corporal was sent up to the Alhambra, under a guard, in his gallows garb, like a hooded friar, but with head erect and a face of iron. The escribano was demanded in exchange, according to the cartel. The once bustling and self-sufficient man of the law was drawn forth from his dungeon more dead than alive. All his flippancy and conceit had evaporated; his hair, it is said, had nearly turned gray with affright, and he had a downcast, dogged look, as if he still felt the halter round his neck.

The old governor stuck his one arm akimbo, and for a moment surveyed him with an iron smile. "Henceforth, my friend," said he, "moderate your zeal in hurrying others to the gallows; be not too certain of your safety, even though you should have the law on your side; and above all take care how you play off your schoolcraft another time upon an old soldier."

The Stage Coach

Omne bene
Sine poena
Tempus est ludendi.
Venit hora
Absque mora
Libros deponendi.
Old Holiday School Song

IN THE course of a December tour in Yorkshire, I rode for a long distance in one of the public coaches, on the day preceding Christmas. The coach was crowded, both inside and out, with passengers, who, by their talk, seemed principally bound to the mansions of relations or friends, to eat the Christmas dinner. It was loaded also with hampers of game, and baskets and boxes of delicacies; and hares hung dangling their long ears about the coachman's box, presents from distant friends for the impending feast. I had three fine rosy-cheeked boys for my fellow-passengers inside, full of the buxom health and manly spirit which I have observed in the children of this country. They were returning home for the holidays in high glee, and promising themselves a world of enjoyment. It was delightful to hear the gigantic plans of the little rogues, and the impracticable feats they were to perform during their six weeks' emancipation from the abhorred thraldom of book, birch, and pedagogue. They were full of anticipations of the meeting with the family and household, down to the very cat and dog; and of the joy they were to give their little sisters by the presents with which their pockets were crammed; but the meeting to which they seemed to look forward with the greatest impatience was with Bantam, which I found to be a pony, and, according to their talk, possessed of more virtues than any steed since the days of Bucephalus. How he could trot! how he could run! and then such leaps as he would take—there was not a hedge in the whole country that he could not clear.

They were under the particular guardianship of the coachman, to whom, whenever an opportunity presented, they addressed a host of questions, and pronounced him one of the best fellows in the world. Indeed, I could not but notice the more than ordinary air of bustle and importance of the coachman, who wore his hat a little on one side, and had a large bunch of Christmas greens stuck in the buttonhole of his coat. He is always a personage full of mighty care and business, but he is particularly so during this season, having so many commissions to execute in consequence of the great interchange of presents. And here, perhaps, it may not be unacceptable to my untravelled readers, to have a sketch that may serve as a general representation of this very numerous and important class of functionaries, who have a dress, a manner, a language, an air, peculiar to themselves, and prevalent throughout the fraternity; so that, wherever an English stage coachman may be seen, he cannot be mistaken for one of any other craft or mystery.

He has commonly a broad, full face, curiously mottled with red, as if the blood had been forced by hard feeding into every vessel of the skin; he is swelled into jolly dimensions by frequent potations of malt liquors, and his bulk is still further increased by a multiplicity of coats, in which he is buried like a cauliflower, the upper one reaching to his heels. He wears a broad-brimmed, low-crowned hat; a huge roll of colored handkerchief about his neck, knowingly knotted and tucked in at the bosom; and has in summer time a large bouquet of flowers in his button-hole; the present, most probably, of some enamored country lass. His waistcoat is commonly of some bright color, striped, and his small clothes extend far below the knees, to meet a pair of jockey boots which reach about half way up his legs.

All this costume is maintained with much precision; he has a pride in having his clothes of excellent materials; and, notwithstanding the seeming grossness of his appearance, there is still discernible that neatness and propriety of person, which is almost inherent in an Englishman. He enjoys great consequence and consideration along the road; has frequent conferences with the village housewives, who look upon him as a man of great trust and dependence; and he seems to have a good understanding with every bright-eyed country lass. The moment he arrives where the horses are to be changed, he throws down the reins with something of an air, and abandons the cattle to the care of the hostler; his duty being merely to drive from one stage to another. When off the box, his hands are thrust into the pockets of his great coat, and he rolls about the inn yard with an air of the most absolute lordliness. Here he is generally surrounded by an admiring throng of hostlers, stable-boys, shoeblacks, and those nameless hangers-on, that infest inns and taverns, and run errands, and do all kind of odd jobs, for the privilege of battening on the drippings of the kitchen and the leakage of the tap-room. These all look up to him as to an oracle; treasure up his cant phrases; echo his opinions about horses and other topics of jockey lore; and, above all, endeavor to imitate his air and carriage. Every ragamuffin that has a coat to his back, thrusts his hands in the pockets, rolls in his gait, talks slang, and is an embryo Coachey.

Perhaps it might be owing to the pleasing serenity that

reigned in my own mind, that I fancied I saw cheerfulness in every countenance throughout the journey. A stage coach, however, carries animation always with it, and puts the world in motion as it whirls along. The horn, sounded at the entrance of a village, produces a general bustle. Some hasten forth to meet friends; some with bundles and band-boxes to secure places, and in the hurry of the moment can hardly take leave of the group that accompanies them. In the meantime, the coachman has a world of small commissions to execute. Sometimes he delivers a hare or pheasant; sometimes jerks a small parcel or newspaper to the door of a public house; and sometimes, with knowing leer and words of sly import, hands to some half-blushing, half-laughing housemaid an odd-shaped billet-doux from some rustic admirer. As the coach rattles through the village, every one runs to the window, and you have glances on every side of fresh country faces and blooming giggling girls. At the corners are assembled juntos of village idlers and wise men, who take their stations there for the important purpose of seeing company pass; but the sagest knot is generally at the blacksmith's, to whom the passing of the coach is an event fruitful of much speculation. The smith, with the horse's heel in his lap, pauses as the vehicle whirls by; the cyclops round the anvil suspend their ringing hammers, and suffer the iron to grow cool; and the sooty spectre, in brown paper cap, laboring at the bellows, leans on the handle for a moment, and permits the asthmatic engine to heave a long-drawn sigh, while he glares through the murky smoke and sulphureous gleams of the smithy.

Perhaps the impending holiday might have given a more than usual animation to the country, for it seemed to me as if everybody was in good looks and good spirits. Game, poultry, and other luxuries of the table, were in brisk circulation in the villages; the grocers', butchers' and fruiterers' shops were thronged with customers. The housewives were stirring briskly about, putting their dwellings in order; and the glossy branches of holly, with their bright-red berries, began to appear at the windows. The scene brought to mind an old writer's account of Christmas preparations:—"Now capons and hens, beside turkeys, geese, and ducks, with beef and mutton—must all die—for in twelve days a multitude of people will not be fed with a little. Now plums and spice, sugar and honey, square it among pies and broth. Now or never must music be in tune, for the youth must dance and sing to get them a heat, while the aged sit by the fire. The country maid leaves half her market, and must be sent again, if she forgets a pack of cards on Christmas eve. Great is the contention of holly and ivy, whether master or dame wears the breeches. Dice and cards benefit the butler; and if the cook do not lack wit, he will sweetly lick his fingers."

I was roused from this fit of luxurious meditation, by a shout from my little travelling companions. They had been looking out of the coach windows for the last few miles, recognizing every tree and cottage as they approached home, and now there was a general burst of joy—"There's John! and there's old Carlo! and there's Bantam!" cried the happy little rogues, clapping their hands.

At the end of a lane there was an old sober-looking servant in livery, waiting for them; he was accompanied by a super-annuated pointer, and by the redoubtable Bantam, a little old rat of a pony, with a shaggy mane and long rusty tail, who stood dozing quietly by the road-side, little dreaming of the bustling times that awaited him.

I was pleased to see the fondness with which the little fellows leaped about the steady old footman, and hugged the pointer; who wriggled his whole body for joy. But Bantam was the great object of interest; all wanted to mount at once, and it was with some difficulty that John arranged that they should ride by turns, and the eldest should ride first.

Off they set at last; one on the pony, with the dog bounding and barking before him, and the others holding John's hands; both talking at once, and overpowering him with questions about home, and with school anecdotes. I looked after them with a feeling in which I do not know whether pleasure or melancholy predominated; for I was reminded of those days when, like them, I had neither known care nor sorrow, and a holiday was the summit of earthly felicity. We stopped a few moments afterwards to water the horses, and on resuming our route, a turn of the road brought us in sight of a neat country seat. I could just distinguish the forms of a lady and two young girls in the portico, and I saw my little comrades, with Bantam, Carlo, and old John, trooping along the carriage road. I leaned out of the coach window, in hopes of witnessing the happy meeting, but a grove of trees shut it from my sight.

In the evening we reached a village where I had determined to pass the night. As we drove into the great gateway of the inn, I saw on one side the light of a rousing kitchen fire beaming through a window. I entered, and admired, for the hundredth time, that picture of convenience, neatness, and broad honest enjoyment, the kitchen of an English inn. It was of spacious dimensions, hung round with copper and tin vessels highly polished, and decorated here and there with a Christmas green. Hams, tongues, and flitches of bacon, were suspended from the ceiling; a smoke-jack made its ceaseless clanking beside the fireplace, and a clock ticked in one corner. A well-scoured deal table extended along one side of the kitchen, with a cold round of beef, and other hearty viands upon it, over which two foaming tankards of ale seemed mounting guard. Travellers of inferior order were preparing to attack this stout repast, while others sat smoking and gossiping over their ale on two high-backed oaken settles beside the fire. Trim housemaids were hurrying backwards and forwards under the directions of a fresh, bustling landlady; but still seizing an occasional moment to exchange a flippant word, and have a rallying laugh, with the group round the fire. The scene completely realized Poor Robin's humble idea of the comforts of mid-winter:

> Now trees their leafy hats do bare
> To reverence Winter's silver hair;
> A handsome hostesss, merry host,
> A pot of ale now and a toast,
> Tobacco and a good coal fire,
> Are things this season doth require.[1]

I had not been long at the inn when a post-chaise drove up to the door. A young gentleman stept out, and by the light of the lamps I caught a glimpse of a countenance which I thought I knew. I moved forward to get a nearer view, when his eye caught mine. I was not mistaken; it was Frank Bracebridge, a sprightly good-humored young fellow, with whom I had once travelled on the continent. Our meeting was extremely cordial, for the countenance of an old fellow-traveller always brings up the recollection of a thousand pleasant scenes, odd adventures, and excellent jokes. To discuss all these in a transient interview at an inn was impossible; and finding that I was not pressed for time, and was merely making a tour of observation, he insisted that I should give him a day or two at his father's country seat, to which he was going to pass the holidays, and which lay at a few miles distance. "It is better than eating a solitary Christmas dinner at an inn," said he, "and I can assure you of a hearty welcome in something of the old-fashioned style." His reasoning was cogent, and I must confess the preparation I had seen for

[1] Poor Robin's Almanac, 1684.

universal festivity and social enjoyment had made me feel a little impatient of my loneliness. I closed, therefore, at once, with his invitation; the chaise drove up to the door, and in a few moments I was on my way to the family mansion of the Bracebridges.